BUILDING BLOCKS OF MURDER

VANESSA GRAY BARTAL

DRY CREEK PRESS

Copyright © 2012, 2021 by Vanessa Gray Bartal

PROLOGUE

"The building, constructed from bricks in nearby Mason County, is slated to be finished before 1890 dawns. Our own Robert Stakely, the building's namesake and financier, assures this reporter that his creation will be a boon for new development downtown._

'The innovation of modern steel technology will make this building the first of its kind in our area,' Stakely is quoted as saying. 'While the exterior will be made of local brick, the frame will be steel, allowing the building to be four stories high—a skyscraper, if you will. This building will never fall.'"

The weathered piece of newspaper fluttered to the floor and another behind it jumped to the forefront.

"Susan Pendergast, a local merchant, was found dead this morning inside the Stakely building. Police have ruled it a homicide and are asking the public for their help in..."

The article was crumpled before being tossed forcefully into the trash can. The newspaper clippings arrived every year like clockwork, and the game was growing old. As if any reminders were needed; as if the day wasn't committed to memory already.

Suddenly, it was too much. At more than twenty years, things had gone on too long already. The lies caused by that long ago day in the Stakely building had built and built so that life itself had become one giant web of intrigue. But what to do? How to solve all the problems at once?

The gun locked safely in the desk drawer beckoned, promising an answer to all life's problems. A gun had started the trouble so long ago, wasn't it poetic justice that a gun end it, too? On the desk was a blank piece of paper, lying there as if waiting patiently to become a murder plot. Trading the gun for a pencil, the paper was soon filled with a plan to solve everything, and this time it would be done right.

CHAPTER 1

"We have a problem."

Lacy Steele looked up from the pile of fancy French underpants she had been sorting. Her friend, Tosh, was studying her with a troubled expression. "Are you referring to the fact that my deceased biological grandmother owned sexier underwear than I've ever even seen?" she asked.

Tosh grimaced. "No, that's your problem. Good luck in therapy. I'm talking about me."

Lacy put down the underwear and gave him her full attention. Tosh rarely spoke about himself. He was a good listener and a caring friend. "What is it?"

"My brother is coming. Here," he added emphatically when she failed to look concerned.

"And that's a problem because…"

He sighed and sat back. "You don't understand. This is my closest brother, both in age and relationship. He's your age, only two years younger. Before I became serious and felt called into the ministry, he and I had some notoriously wild times. He doesn't approve of my chosen vocation. He's been disappointed in me since I became a pastor."

"I would think he would appreciate the fact that, by becoming an protestant minister, you rebelled against your Catholic roots," she said.

"You would think that. But the irony is that he's incredibly loyal to the church. So, to him, becoming a protestant pastor is a double betrayal."

"And that's why you're upset that he's coming here?" she asked.

"No. Our disagreement has been raging for years. The problem is that he sort of thinks we're dating."

"Tosh, you told him we're dating?" she asked.

"Of course not," he said. "That would have been a lie. He arrived at the idea on his own."

"How?" she asked, suspicious now.

"Well, he was sort of giving me a hard time about moving to a town where I brought the median age of the population down to eighty. I told him there was a young woman here I had been spending time with. He asked if you were hot, and I told him yes." He paused to smile at her, waiting to see if she was pleased by the statement. His smile slipped when her expression remained neutral. He cleared his throat. "So anyway, then he said 'Wow, Tosh, I can't believe you moved to a new town and found a girlfriend on the first day.'"

"And what was your response to that?"

"Um, I believe it was uncomfortable laughter and a topic change."

"Tosh," she exclaimed.

"Well, you have to admit our relationship is sort of confusing, Lacy. We spend a lot of time together, don't we?"

"Yes," she agreed.

"And we've kissed."

"Once. Briefly."

"Okay, but my point is that we're not exactly strangers. We're sort of caught between, wouldn't you say?"

"Was law your second career choice? Because I think you'd be a shoo-in for Ed McNeil's second chair." Ed McNeil was the lawyer who had gotten Lacy's grandmother out of jail after she was arrested for murder.

"Why *aren't* we dating?" Tosh asked.

"You said you wanted to take things slowly because of your position in the community," she reminded him.

"Slow and stopped are two different things," he said.

She stared uncomfortably at the pile of underpants between them.

"Admit it, Lacy, we both know we're not together because of him," Tosh said.

Lacy looked up. "Jason and I haven't spoken in two weeks."

"And why is that?" Tosh tipped his head and studied her. "What happened between you two?"

Lacy didn't answer. She didn't want to remember the tumultuous kiss she and Jason had shared, the way she had thrown herself at him, and then the way she had flown from the house in a panic after the kiss was over.

"Suspenseful silence doesn't make me any less curious," Tosh said.

"I've been busy," Lacy hedged, and it was partially true. Two weeks ago she had learned that the woman she had always thought was her grandmother wasn't her grandmother at all. Since then, she had discovered that she was her biological grandmother's sole heir. Now she found herself not only sorting through some very mixed emotions, but also trying to sort through Barbara Blake's belongings as well. What was she to do with the designer clothes and shoes that cost more than the house was worth? And what of the million-dollar bank account?

So far Lacy hadn't spent any of the money. After learning the type of woman Barbara had been, Lacy wasn't sure she wanted anything to do with her, not even the large sum of money gathering dust in some bank.

"Have you called Riley back?" Tosh asked. Absently he began to sort the pile on the floor before realizing with a grimace that he was touching a strange woman's underpants. He wiped his hand on his shirt and sat back on his heels, awaiting Lacy's answer.

Lacy sighed. If there was one thing she wanted to talk about less than Jason, it was her younger sister, Riley. "No," she said.

"I wasn't pressuring you to do so," Tosh said with a sweet smile. He reached out, clasped her hand, and gave it a squeeze. "I'm on your side, Lacy."

She smiled and returned the gentle pressure of his hand. Taking her gesture as a sign of encouragement, he scooted around the pile of lingerie between them and put his arms around her. She rested her head on his chest, thinking how much her life had changed since she met him. Unbelievably that had only been a few weeks ago. What had she done before Tosh?

Ever since her fiancé dumped her for her little sister, Lacy had felt like her heart was in tatters. Moving from New York back to her tiny hometown had been a difficult, yet necessary, step in her recovery. Here she wasn't faced with daily reminders or sightings of Robert. Her grandmother's loving indulgence was another soothing balm, and now there was Tosh. He cared. He understood.

They sat in comfortable silence a few minutes.

"I should go," Tosh said at last. "It's bingo night." He was the pastor of her grandmother's church and, as such, was in charge of the weekly cutthroat bingo session. "Are you going to be okay here?"

"I'm leaving, too," Lacy declared. There was only so much time and energy she could devote to sorting Barbara's belongings before she became exhausted and overwhelmed. The many unresolved piles all over the house bore testament to that fact.

"You could move in here," Tosh said suddenly. "That would give you more time to sort, and also more privacy."

"I love living with Grandma," Lacy said. She and her grandmother had always been close. Learning they weren't biologically related had done nothing to change that. Plus there was the fact that her grandmother cooked for her every day. Lacy couldn't imagine how lonely it would be to live alone and eat all her meals by herself.

"Maybe your grandma wants some privacy now that she has a boyfriend," Tosh said.

Lacy hadn't thought of that. Her grandmother was now dating Mr. Middleton, Lacy's biological grandfather. Lacy was enjoying the opportunity to get to know him better, but maybe the feeling wasn't mutual. Maybe the older couple wanted some privacy to explore their newfound romance. Somehow the thought that her grandparents might consider her a nuisance was intensely painful to Lacy. She withdrew from Tosh and sat with her hands resting in her lap, staring at the blank wall across from her.

"Uh-oh, you got all quiet. That usually means I said something insensitive," Tosh said.

"I guess I never really thought of myself as being in the way before," Lacy said.

"You're not in the way," Tosh said. "Of course they want to be with you, Lacy. Who wouldn't? You're sweet, and adorable, and…I was just thinking out loud. You should know by now not to listen to half of what I say."

"Yes, but usually the other half is good advice," she said. "Maybe it is time I moved out. I can't ride on Grandma's emotional coattails forever. At some point I need to rejoin the real world and be a grownup again."

Tosh glanced around the house. "This place could look really good with a few updates."

Lacy bit her lip and looked up at him. "Tosh, when I move, I'm moving away. I'm not staying here."

He blinked at her in astonishment. "Are you going back to New York?"

She winced. "No, definitely not."

"Then where?"

That question brought her up short. She had complete freedom to go anywhere now. Where should she go? There were only three places in the world she knew people: New York, her parents' retirement community in Florida, and here—her tiny hometown.

"It's not like you have to decide right now," Tosh added hurriedly. He looked a little panicked over the possibility that she might soon disappear. Not that she could blame him. He hadn't been exaggerating about the geriatric population in their town. Seemingly she, Jason, and Tosh were the only people in town who didn't receive a social security check.

Tosh checked his watch. "I should go." Leaning forward, he pressed a light kiss to her forehead. "Want to walk out with me?"

"I'm going to stay and close up." She patted his chest. "You go ahead. Thanks for keeping me company today, Tosh."

She remained seated on the floor, watching Tosh as he let himself out. He paused at the threshold to give her a smile and a wave, and then he was gone.

The house felt quiet and empty without him and Lacy was disconcerted by her loneliness. She had always prided herself on her ability to enjoy her own company. An introvert by nature, she had never shied away from being by herself. After having a constant stream of roommates, first in college and then in Manhattan, privacy had become something she treasured.

But now, faced with the possibility of moving out of her grandmother's house, Lacy found she was almost afraid to be alone. She told herself it was because she had nowhere to go. She couldn't stay in this town, and even if she wanted to, the house she had inherited wasn't ready. There were too many piles to sort, and it was woefully outdated.

The truth, however, was that she was afraid to be alone. Alone she would have no choice but to deal with all the emotions she had been avoiding, emotions brought on by the double betrayal of her sister and fiancé, emotions brought on by learning that her biological grandmother had been a man-eating user, hated by all and mourned by none.

With a heavy sigh, she shoved the pile of underpants away and stood up. "Creepy," she muttered as she glanced at the underwear. She needed to get away from this house before she became any more depressed, but as soon as she gathered her purse, the doorbell rang. Lacy stood on her toes to see out the door's window. A large woman with broad shoulders and a short haircut stood on the other side.

"Hello, I'm Sheila Whitaker from the Society of American Downtowns. If you have a moment, I would like to talk to you about helping our cause." Her voice was husky, somewhere between masculine and feminine, and she spoke forcefully, with authority.

Lacy looked at the business card the woman had given her, trying not to laugh at the unfortunate acronym for the SAD. "I was just going out," Lacy said, giving a pointed glance toward the driveway. Belatedly she remembered that she had walked from her grandmother's house, so there was no car to stare at, only empty pavement.

"This will only take a moment," Sheila said plaintively.

Lacy suppressed a sigh and sagged in defeat against the doorframe. Taking her dejected pose as encouragement, Sheila began to speak. Lacy only listened with half an ear until she heard a familiar name.

"Wait, what did you say?" Lacy asked, standing straight.

"I said a group of developers wants to tear down the Stakely building," Sheila repeated. The excitement level in her tone notched up at having finally caught Lacy's interest.

"But that place is beautiful," Lacy said. The Stakely building was a huge four story brick building in the center of town. It was one of the oldest and most architecturally interesting buildings in the tiny town. As a young girl, Lacy had found it artistically inspiring. She could almost credit the massive structure with her career choice. Imagining the many stories that could take place in the Stakely building had no doubt shaped Lacy as a writer. "Why do they want to tear it down?"

"They want to put up a strip mall," Sheila said, her tone derisive. "One of those plain cinderblock buildings with a metal roof and neon signs."

Lacy's jaw dropped. "That's horrible. That will ruin what little downtown we have. Surely the town council and mayor won't go along with that."

Sheila barked a harsh laugh. "Oh, sweetheart, you're too new or too young to know much about the politics in this town. Money talks, and the developers are throwing around a whole bunch of money. My effort to try and save the Stakely building is a last-ditch longshot unless I can gain some major support." She tipped her head to the side and gave Lacy an up and down critical inspection. "Having young people at the meeting might go a long way in swaying the council. I think they're under the belief that young people only want what's new and modern and that's what will draw kids back here again."

Lacy frowned as she studied the card in her hand again. "When is the meeting?"

"Tonight at seven at the town hall. Please come, and bring as many young people as you can find."

With that, Sheila steamrolled to the next house in the neighborhood. Lacy wondered if the older woman thought she knew of some secret hangout where all the "young people" in town hid during the day. As far as Lacy knew, she made up one-third of the young demographic. But why was that? Why was their town dying? And what could be done to bring it back to life?

Those questions kept her mind busy on the short walk back to her grandmother's house. When she arrived home, she found her grandfather sitting in the living room waiting for her grandmother to finish getting ready. Lacy smiled at the picture he made, like a real suitor waiting for his girlfriend. Absently she wondered if she should play the role of the strict relative who imposed curfew rules for her grandma, but the thought of telling her former high school principal to have his date home early was too embarrassing to contemplate.

"Hi," Lacy said when she bounded into the house. She hadn't yet worked up the nerve to call him "Grandpa," but "Mr. Middleton" felt too formal. Most of the time, she avoided the topic by not addressing him by name at all.

"Hi, Lacy," her grandfather said. He turned stiffly toward her and smiled.

"Are you sore?" she asked, noting the rigid set of his shoulders.

"Just my arthritis acting up. If I were one of those boring old men who talked about the weather, I would tell you it's going to rain soon."

"I'm ready." Lucinda Craig made the announcement as she stepped into the room. Her eyes were fastened on Mr. Middleton, and they were alive in a way Lacy had never seen them.

She's in love, Lacy thought with a combination of pleasure and envy.

Mr. Middleton labored to his feet. "I was just talking to Lacy."

Lacy's grandmother snapped to attention. "Oh, yes, hi, Lacy," she said, clearly flustered and embarrassed by the raw display of emotion on her face.

"Hi, Grandma," Lacy said. She glanced around the room to give her grandmother time to compose herself. She had no idea why her grandmother had so much trouble revealing her thoughts and emotions to others. Maybe it was a generational thing. Whatever the reason, Lacy was thankful she didn't seem to be holding herself away from Mr. Middleton.

The doorbell rang, providing Lacy with an opportunity to take a step back and answer.

Jason stood on the other side, smiling devilishly. "Hey, Red, I think it's time we talked about that kiss."

CHAPTER 2

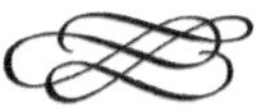

Behind Lacy, Mr. Middleton purposefully cleared his throat. Jason had the good sense to look sheepish.

"So, you're not alone," he said.

"No, she isn't," Mr. Middleton said. Apparently he suffered no compunctions about playing the role of the strict relative. Lacy wondered if he was about to tell Jason to have her home early or something else out of the, *So You're Dating My Granddaughter* handbook.

"Hi, Mr. Middleton," Jason said, pivoting around Lacy and stepping inside. "Hello, Mrs. Craig."

"Hello, Jason." The two older adults spoke as a unit, although Lacy's grandmother was smiling pleasantly and her grandfather was frowning.

Lucinda came forward and laid a hand on Mr. Middleton's bicep. "Tom, hadn't we better get going?"

"I don't know," he muttered darkly, his sharp gaze shooting between Lacy and Jason. Lacy resisted the urge to squirm under his inspection.

"We should go," Lucinda reaffirmed. "You kids take care." She took

Mr. Middleton's hand and began tugging as she walked toward the door.

Reluctantly, he followed her, but when he reached the door, he paused and turned back to Jason. "Remember that time your junior year I found you and Madison Thompson behind the stage during sixth period?"

"Yes," Jason said. Lacy had never heard his voice crack before.

"I'd better not find you that way with my granddaughter. Ever." With that, he turned and walked out of the house, closing the door firmly behind him.

Lacy wanted to ask exactly how he had been found with Madison Thompson, but as soon as her grandparents left the house, so did her courage. There was a reason she hadn't spoken to him in the two weeks since they kissed; she had no idea what to say.

Jason, however, seemed immensely relieved when the door closed. He turned to Lacy with a grin. "Mr. Middleton never gets any less scary, you know? He's like the Paul Rudd of principals—ageless."

Lacy stared blankly at him until his smile slipped.

"C'mon, Lacy, you're not still mad at me, are you?"

That provoked a reply. "Mad at you? Why would I be mad at you?"

"Because I kissed you. You said no kissing or we couldn't be friends."

"You didn't kiss me; I kissed you," she argued.

"That's not how I remember it," Jason said. "You were crying, and I kissed you to make you feel better."

"No." Lacy shook her head. "I was crying and I kissed you to make myself feel better."

"And then you ran away."

She looked away then, searching for anything other than his face to focus on. "I had to. I was embarrassed."

"Why were you embarrassed? It was a good kiss, great even. Shakespeare could have written sonnets about that kiss." He paused and now it was his turn to look down. "I haven't been able to stop thinking about it, actually."

That drew her attention back to him. "Really?" She hadn't made a total fool of herself? She hadn't sent him screaming for cover by blatantly throwing herself at him?

He looked up and their eyes locked. "Really."

The air between them crackled for a few beats, and then she was in his arms with no recollection of how she got there. His hands grasped her biceps while his head dipped toward her, but then he paused.

"Should we be doing this?" he asked. "Don't we need to talk about it first?"

"When did you become a girl?" she asked. "No talking; just kiss me."

He smiled. "Yes, ma'am," he said, and then he kissed her.

He was much taller than she, and the height difference made kissing while standing awkward, especially when she was wearing flat-heeled sneakers as she was today. She pressed him against the back of the couch behind him, vaguely urging him to sit down. But when he bumped the couch, he overbalanced. Toppling backward, he latched onto her to try to right himself, not realizing that since she was smaller she would simply fall with him.

Together, they somersaulted over the couch, bumped into the coffee table, scattered a stack of newspapers into the air, and landed hard on the floor with Jason solidly on top of Lacy, his shoulder smashing her face.

"Are you okay?" he said when he found enough air to speak.

"I think so," she replied, her voice muffled against his shirt. He shimmied down in order to free her face so that when he spoke again they were nose to nose.

"Please tell me that little incident wasn't actually your plan when you backed me into the couch."

"I wanted to sit down, but you should know up front my plans never work out so well." She smiled. He smiled. She closed her eyes and tipped her face up to receive his kiss, but it never came. When she opened her eyes a few seconds later, she realized a headline from one of the newspapers had caught his attention.

His lips moved as he silently read the words, and then he rolled off her and snatched up the paper. Lacy peered over her shoulder and smiled self-consciously when she read her own name.

"What is this?" Jason asked. He held out the paper in her direction and looked up.

"I've been freelancing for the paper," Lacy said, fighting a blush. Though the article had originally been intended for their small town's local paper, it had been picked up by a wire service before quickly going national. Lacy's name was now in some of the largest papers in the country, and her grandparents had bought them all, which was why so many papers were now scattered around the living room after Jason and Lacy crashed into them.

"Are you kidding me?" Jason asked, incredulous.

Lacy was just about to reassure him her newly attained notoriety was no big deal, but then he continued.

"Are you insane? I can't believe you would do this to me."

She sat up and scooted away from him and he did the same so there were now two feet between them. "What are you talking about? I didn't do anything to you."

"Really? Because I would call writing a scathing article about the sheriff's department a pretty lousy thing to do to me."

"Jason," she implored. "The article has nothing to do with you. It's all about Detective Brenner and his incompetence."

"No, Lacy, it's not. It's a reflection on the entire department and it makes us all look like a bunch of hick yokel bumbling idiots. This article does nothing but reinforce the stereotype of the ignorant small-town cop." He finished speaking and threw the paper down in disgust.

"It does no such thing," Lacy argued. She picked the paper up and tapped it for emphasis. "This isn't simply about how he mishandled my grandmother's case. I went back for the last few years since he's been head detective and found a whole handful of cases that he mishandled."

Jason slapped his palm to his forehead. "That's what the subpoena was about."

"What subpoena?" she asked.

"The subpoena I received today about an old closed case from years ago when I first started on the force. I caught and arrested the bad guy, but Detective Brenner was the officer in charge of the case. Now, thanks to you, lawyers are going to have a heyday reopening all the old cases and letting guilty men go free."

"That's not going to happen," Lacy said with slightly less conviction.

"Don't be naïve, Lacy. That's exactly what's going to happen. You could have filed a formal complaint against Brenner and opened an official investigation into his handling of your grandmother's case but, no, you had to vet your issues in a national forum and now my entire department is going to get dragged through the mud. And everyone is going to blame me because you're my...because we..." He broke off with a disgusted grunt before jumping nimbly to his feet.

Lacy also dashed to her feet, although far less gracefully. "Why are you taking this so personally? This has nothing to do with you and everything to do with him."

"Why am I taking this personally? Because it is personal, Lacy. This is my job, my life. It wasn't enough that you had to stick your nose in your grandmother's case and almost get yourself killed, but now you're sticking your finger in cases that are none of your business. Do you have any idea how much trouble you've caused?"

"If Detective Brenner's bumbling has put even one innocent person in jail and this investigation helps make him free, then it will all be worth it."

Jason pressed his palms to his eye sockets and groaned. "You and your ideals."

"Yes, me and my ideals," she said. "Don't you want to see justice served? Don't you want to see the innocent protected?"

He dropped his hands from his eyes and gave her a weary look. "What about me? I'm innocent, but now I'm going to be dragged through the mud until the mess you've caused gets cleared up."

"That's not going to happen," she assured him. "You're a good cop, Jason, and everyone knows it." Her hand reached out to rest on his forearm, but he took a step back.

"Don't, just don't. I can't deal with this right now."

"You mean you can't deal with me right now," she said.

He didn't deny it. Instead, he turned and let himself quietly out the door.

What just happened here? How had things gone so quickly from kissing to yelling? Lacy shook her head and headed for the kitchen. Really, she wasn't any worse off with Jason than she had been before the encounter, except now she knew for sure he was upset with her. She could only hope that, given time, he might cool off and think rationally. When the hubbub her article had caused piped down and nothing bad happened to Jason or the department, he would realize Lacy had been correct. Or, at the very least, maybe he wouldn't hate her anymore.

She ate a lonely supper of reheated leftovers while watching the news on television. What was wrong with her life that her grandmother was on a hot date while she, Lacy, sat eating reheated meatloaf and watching a segment about obesity in farm animals?

There was no excuse not to go to the SAD meeting at the town hall, but she didn't want to go alone. Knowing Tosh wouldn't be able to answer his phone during the middle of an all-important bingo event, she texted him and asked him to meet her there when bingo was over.

In addition to Sheila, there were a handful of angry-looking elderly people at the meeting. Lacy sat in the back, but Sheila still whipped her head around to smile in delight at her appearance. Lacy smiled self-consciously in return, and the meeting came to order.

For the first half hour, mundane town business was discussed. Lacy wished she had brought a book to read as the mayor spent a long time extolling the virtues of the new street salt supplier the city would be using in the winter. Lacy had no idea anyone could talk so long or so lovingly about salt.

Just as she began to despair of staying awake long enough to talk about the Stakely building, Tosh slipped into the seat beside her, and Sheila took the floor.

"Mayor, council members, I respectfully ask you to refrain from tearing down the Stakely building." After that opening parry, she began extolling the virtues of the Stakely building, beginning with its history. After hearing the building had been constructed in the late eighteen hundreds and used as a candy factory, Lacy was even more intrigued.

"And so I implore you not to lose this historic treasure." Sheila finished speaking and scanned the faces of the town council behind her. Lacy did the same, and was disheartened by what she saw. Without exception, all of them looked bored and resolute. She knew then that the decision to tear it down was a foregone conclusion and they had simply been humoring Sheila.

"Well, that was a fine speech, Sheila," Mayor Watkins began. "But as I told you, we've already voted. The building will be sold, and the developers can do what they want with it."

Lacy gasped. "That's terrible," she whispered to Tosh. "They're not even listening. Someone needs to say something."

"Don't look at me," he said. "I'm a new pastor in this community; I'm not getting involved in local politics."

Before she could talk herself out of it, Lacy shot to her feet. The council looked at her in surprise. Sheila beamed.

"Please, you can't tear down the Stakely building," she blurted. "Don't you realize it's the epicenter of our downtown, the only thing that gives us distinction? A strip mall would take away the one piece of character we have going for us."

Disconcerted murmurs rippled through the crowd. The mayor gave a hushing glare around the room.

"Young lady, I can't possibly expect you to understand the finer points of business. The wheels of progress must sometimes be greased with pain. I understand that some have a certain attachment to the Stakely building, but it's a behemoth. The cost to renovate it, let alone keep up on it, is more than anyone is willing to pay. Right now we have a company that wants to buy it and put in profitable businesses that could bring jobs to our community. Why should we say no to that?"

"Because as a town we would be selling our souls." The audience gasped. Lacy wondered if this was as much excitement as a town council meeting had ever produced. "Can't you understand that by taking the easy road, we would be cutting off our noses to spite our faces? Yes, some cheap stores will filter in when the strip mall comes, but the jobs they bring will be minimum wage at best, and the clientele those establishments attract will make the downtown a red light district."

The mayor wasn't listening, Lacy could tell. He shook his head obstinately and gave her a patronizing smile. "I couldn't possibly expect you to understand the ins and outs of business. We have an offer on the table, and good business sense tells us to accept it."

Lacy slumped into her chair, angrier than she had been in a long time. She hated condescension, either because of her age or her gender, and the mayor seemed to be employing both in one fell swoop.

"Someone should do something," she muttered. "Someone should buy that building."

Tosh leaned over to whisper in her ear. "Uh, Lacy, you're a millionaire."

Lacy sat up in alarm and looked at Tosh. She had completely forgotten about Barbara Blake's money. Could she do this? Could she buy this building and save it?

She shot to her feet once again. The mayor tried to ignore her, but she spoke anyway. "How much are the developers going to pay for the Stakely building?"

The mayor ignored her, but Sheila spoke up. "A hundred and fifty thousand."

"That's it?" Lacy asked, incredulous.

Sheila nodded sadly. "We've raised some support to try and buy it ourselves, but everything has happened so suddenly we only have a few thousand dollars."

Lacy hesitated. Should she really do what she was thinking? Tosh nudged her, urging her into action. "I'll buy it," she announced before she could change her mind.

That got everyone's attention. The mayor finally looked at her with a frown. "There's no time for you to go through the process of trying to get a loan, if you could even get one, which I doubt."

"I don't need a loan," Lacy said. "I'll pay for it in cash." She tipped her chin stubbornly, aware that she was treading on dangerous ground when her pride had been lanced.

Now the mayor looked flustered. "But we've already agreed to sell to the developers."

"Have papers been signed? Has money changed hands?" Lacy pressed.

"Well, no, but we have a gentleman's agreement," the mayor hedged.

"There are no gentlemen in business," Lacy said, trying to sound like she knew what she was talking about. "You have nothing legal from them, and I'm offering to sign the papers tonight. And, really, do you want people to know that you turned down a chance to save the Stakely building in favor of outsiders who are going to tear it down?"

Behind the mayor, the council members were wavering.

"You let this go, Hal, and I'll make sure everyone knows," Sheila threatened.

Reluctantly, the mayor agreed, and just like that Lacy owned a building.

She signed the papers in dismay, having no idea how such a thing came about. Tosh hovered approvingly in the background, handing her a pen whenever the need arose.

"That was awesome," he said as they finally exited the building late that night after all the bureaucracy had been handled. "I can't believe you were like, 'I'll buy your building.' Take that, city council!"

Lacy pressed her fingertips to her throbbing temples. "I can't believe I just did that." She spun and studied the town hall. "Do you think it's too late to back out?"

Tosh took her hand and steered her once again toward the parking lot. "What's the big deal? You bought a building. My family buys buildings all the time. My dad says real estate is always a good investment."

"My family doesn't buy buildings all the time. We buy a house when we can afford the down payment and spend the next thirty years paying it off." Lacy stopped and bent over, sucking oxygen. "I can't believe I just did that. I think I'm going to be sick."

Tosh pressed his palm to her back. "Lacy, it's no big deal. You could have bought ten of those buildings with what you have in the bank. If you don't want to keep it, just find another buyer and resell it."

How could she explain to a trust-fund baby the dynamics of growing up middle class? She couldn't, she realized. While Tosh was down to earth on many levels, he had no grasp of finances. He had no concept of how most people lived week to week, paycheck to paycheck, just hoping to get ahead. Before Lacy's inheritance came through, she'd had exactly three hundred dollars to her name.

"Let me drive you home," Tosh volunteered.

But as they took a step toward the parking lot, a body suddenly hurled itself at Lacy, knocking her backwards against the wall.

CHAPTER 3

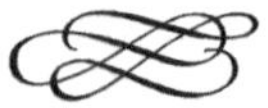

"Sorry, did I hurt you?" Sheila Whitaker asked as she released Lacy from a bear hug. "I'm just so happy." Without giving her time to answer her previous question, she grabbed Lacy's hands in a death grip and continued speaking. "Listen, I know it feels like we're alone in this fight, but we're not. We have friends. Big, important friends." Her tone was cryptic, as was the narrow-eyed look she was giving Lacy. With one final, painful squeeze of Lacy's hands, Sheila turned and walked away.

"That was…weird," Tosh whispered.

Lacy nodded. "Do you think she was a marine?" How else to explain her bone-crushing strength?

"Are we sure she's always been a woman?"

"Tosh," Lacy exclaimed. She lightly shoved his arm, and he laughed.

"What? She has a very masculine energy."

"Sometimes I have a really hard time believing you're someone's pastor."

"Not hers," Tosh said. "Otherwise I wouldn't be able to make fun of her." He looped his arm around Lacy's neck and gave her a playful squeeze. They walked in companionable silence to his car, and then he drove her home. He turned off his car, and they sat in comfortable silence a few minutes.

"So, my brother's coming tomorrow. Are you free for dinner?"

"We don't have to pretend to be a couple or anything, do we?" Lacy asked.

"I won't lie to him, Lacy." Tosh fidgeted with a keychain. "Although, if we were a couple, we wouldn't be lying."

Lacy squinted at the large maple tree in her grandmother's front yard. Was it her imagination, or were the leaves beginning to fall early this year? "I don't know, Tosh. I don't think I'm ready for a relationship. I'm still in recovery mode."

"Maybe you won't know until you try," Tosh suggested.

Lacy shrugged.

"That's an underwhelming response," Tosh said. He hunched in his seat and stared hard at the maple tree, too.

"You're not allowed to be angry with me. I told you up front how it is."

"I'm not angry," Tosh said sullenly. He perked up and smiled at her, leaning across the seat to kiss her cheek. "Promise, I'm not angry." He bussed her cheek a second time and started his car. "I'll pick you up at six tomorrow. I won't pretend we're anything more than friends to my brother, but if you could wear something knockout and fawn all over me, that would be great."

"I'll see what I can do," she promised. "See you tomorrow."

He waited in the driveway until she was safely inside, and then he drove away.

As soon as she stepped inside, she saw her grandparents sitting together on the couch, their heads close together in conversation. They turned to her with smiles when she entered the room.

"Hi, honey, were you out with Jason?" her grandmother asked.

"No, I was with Tosh. I bought a building." She sat heavily on the chair opposite them, her legs suddenly numb with renewed shock.

Her grandparents blinked at her in unison as if their eyelids were working in coordination. "You what?" Mr. Middleton asked.

"I bought the Stakely building," she said.

He took a sip of his coffee before answering. "I always liked that building. What are you going to do with it?"

His matter-of-fact attitude made Lacy smile, easing some of her anxiety. "I have no idea. What do you guys think I should do?"

"That's up to you, honey," her grandmother said. She sat back with a nostalgic smile. "Lots of good memories happened at that building. Remember, Tom, when it was a happening marketplace?" Her hand rested on his forearm.

Now it was Mr. Middleton's turn to smile. "Those were good days. The town was bustling and not everyone was old and dried up."

"I didn't know it was ever a marketplace," Lacy said.

"It closed when you were a baby," her grandmother replied.

"What was it like?" she asked. She sat back as her grandparents began to regale her with tales of what the town had been like fifty years ago. As they talked, a picture began to form in her mind. Wouldn't it be great if the Stakely building could be returned to its former glory? The thought that she had no idea how to embark on such an adventure tried to intrude, but she wouldn't let it. Where there was a will there was a way, right? How hard could it be to renovate a one-hundred-year-old building?

"I'm supposed to look at it tomorrow with the inspector," Lacy said when their reminiscence was finished. "Will you go with me?" she asked her grandfather. Maybe it was an old-fashioned notion, but she believed all men were endowed with the ability to know things about construction, whereas she knew nothing at all.

"Love to," he said. His tone didn't change, but she knew he was pleased by her request. For so many years, he had been alone, standing on the periphery of their family and looking in. Lacy felt bad about all those wasted years; she was anxious to make up for them by including him in her life as much as possible. Plus, she genuinely liked him. Like her grandmother, he was a kind, wise, and no-nonsense person.

"It's a date, then," she said, standing. "Good night you two." *Don't stay up too late,* she was tempted to add. Even though she yawned on the way to her bedroom, she had trouble falling asleep. The day had been eventful, to say the least. She had bought a building. Tosh's brother was coming to town, and he thought she and Tosh were dating. Most of all, though, her mind kept replaying the earlier scene with Jason. And even though the fight had been ugly, her thoughts dwelled mostly on what had happened before the yelling began.

Why did being in his arms have to feel so good? And why did he have to be so very beautiful? Most of all, why should she care about either of those things? Telling Tosh she wasn't ready for a relationship had almost become a mantra, and yet every time she was near Jason, she lost her head.

Don't lose your heart, too, was the last sleepy warning she gave herself before she finally drifted off to sleep.

* * *

The morning brought amnesia until the building inspector called Lacy to confirm their appointment. Then the memory of buying a building, plus her anxiety over the subject, returned full force. She spent a moment in self-recrimination before pulling up her figurative bootstraps. What was done was done; she might as well face the matter head on and figure out what needed to be done next.

She showered, taking the time to blow dry her hair and apply makeup. Perhaps it didn't make sense, but looking good made her feel more capable and in control of her circumstances. Maybe if she looked like she had it all together someone might believe she actually did.

Her grandfather showed up as she and her grandmother were finishing breakfast. He waved her grandmother away when she rose to pour him a mug of coffee. Pouring his own coffee, he sat at the table between the two women.

"Seen the paper today?" he asked.

Lacy wasn't fooled by his bland tone. She was beginning to know him. The more he suppressed his emotions, the more emotional he was feeling. "No, what is it?"

He blew on the coffee, stalling for time, and then he answered. "An old case is being reopened."

She wondered if it was the same case Jason had referred to. "Jason told me about that, I think."

Mr. Middleton nodded. "He was the arresting officer."

"What type of case was it?" Lacy asked.

"Murder," he answered.

She gasped. "Not…not Barbara Blake's murder." She bit her lip and looked uncertainly at her grandmother. Peggy, the woman who had murdered Barbara Blake, had confessed to the crime, sparing them all the horror of a trial.

"No. This is an old murder from a quarter century ago."

Lacy frowned, puzzled. "But Jason has only been on the force for seven years." After high school, he received a two year associate's degree before joining their local sheriff's department. Most rookies began their careers in the jail, like her friend, Travis, but Jason had shown such promise that he bypassed that step and became a road unit.

"It was an old unsolved case that became solved shortly after he began working there."

Lacy's frown deepened. "He was so new; surely reopening the case couldn't affect him, could it, Gra…" She broke off, stopping herself before she could call him "Grandpa." A blush rose to warm her cheeks, and she immediately felt awkward for her bumbling mistake. Why couldn't she bite the bullet and use the endearment? Though they weren't biologically related, Lacy was too much like her Grandma Lucinda. They both had trouble expressing their emotions.

Mr. Middleton paused, but Lacy thought it was because he was measuring his words and not because he had noticed any awkwardness on her part. "There are things you don't know about Jason, Lacy," he said at last.

"Like what?" she asked.

He took another sip of coffee. "Not my place to say."

Now it was her turn to sip her coffee, and she did so thoughtfully. As their former principal, Mr. Middleton had access to information about everyone, but what could he know about Jason? By his tone, she guessed it was something bad, but she could never believe anything bad about Jason. His character was unimpeachable. Even if he sometimes ran short on mercy, he retained an overdeveloped sense of justice.

"We should go," her grandfather said, jarring her out of her brooding thoughts. They both kissed her grandmother's cheek, and then they were off. The building inspector, Kerry March, was waiting for them, even though they were a few minutes early.

"I like to show up early and begin my inspection of the outside," he explained when Lacy apologized for arriving after him. She wondered if he would comment about the building, but he didn't. She felt oddly insulted by his lack of comment on her new building. How exciting must his job be if the sight of the Stakely building did nothing to impress him? On the other hand, maybe he was one of those businessmen who was strictly business while the time clock was ticking.

The trio stood back to survey the outside of the building. It looked good to Lacy, but what did she know? Nothing, which was why her grandfather and Mr. March were there. She ran her hand lovingly over the bricks, remembering with a smile some of the many stories she had created about the old building. A budding sense of happiness began to well in her chest. Maybe her hasty decision wasn't all bad. After all, she had a true affection for the place. This could be the start of something good.

"Shall we?" Mr. March asked. Some of Lacy's enthusiasm dimmed when he handed a construction helmet to her before passing one to her grandfather.

"Is the building unsafe?" she asked, taking a timid glance at the structure.

"You never know, but it's over a hundred years old. Better safe than sorry until we know what we're working with," he replied as she donned the ugly hat.

The electricity wasn't on inside the building, but it had several large windows and it was a sunny day. Along with Mr. March's industrial-strength flashlight, there wouldn't be much they couldn't see, unless there was a basement. If there was a basement, Lacy wasn't sure she wanted to find out. What had looked promising outside now looked menacing inside. Everything looked worn, as if it truly were in danger of collapsing on their heads. And spider webs were everywhere, the kind that Hollywood set designers created for haunted houses in the movies. Moving closer to Mr. Middleton, she finally gave up trying to be brave and hooked her arm through his elbow. He gave her arm a light squeeze, and she felt reassured by his presence.

They followed slowly behind Mr. March as he stopped at various points, got down on his knees, and made notes on his pad. Lacy never had any idea what he was looking at. After a few minutes, she gave up trying to figure out if his grunts meant good news, bad news, or arthritis in his joints. Instead she amused herself by looking around the space. As soon as she was able to get over the initial dumpy appearance, she began to see the potential.

The first two floors were joined together and open to make one huge space, ideal for the marketplace her grandparents had talked about. The second floor only had a walkway, leaving the middle open, almost like some modern malls she had seen. From above, anyone could see down below, and vice versa, but there were still two floors of store space. If she closed her eyes, she could almost hear the bustle of activity. The architectural details didn't stop on the outside—they were everywhere. Crown molding, stone gargoyles, buttresses, and arches abounded the interior. Perhaps the style was eclectic, but it suited Lacy whose own decorating style was somewhat schizophrenic.

After the grandeur of the first two floors, the third floor was boring in comparison. There was a long corridor with five offices lining each side of the hallway for a total of ten offices. Inside, each office was spacious and equipped with its own bathroom. If she had to guess, she would say at some point someone had tried to remodel this floor to make it useable. Some of the décor in the bathrooms smacked of the 1970's.

The fourth floor was one massive space. There were support beams scattered throughout, but there were no interior walls. The windows were floor to ceiling, and light streamed in, revealing hardwood floors. Lacy's imagination ran away with her as she imagined a ballroom with happy dancing couples floating by.

The inspection took almost three hours. By the time it was finished, Lacy and Mr. Middleton were flagging. They cleared a space in the middle of the first floor by overturning some empty crates, and then they sat down to wait for the final results.

Lacy nervously nibbled her thumb before remembering she had touched all manner of germs in this mausoleum. If the scrabbling of tiny rodent paws was any indication, she could probably give herself the hanta virus by putting her hands in her mouth.

Mr. March came into view and Lacy jumped to her feet. "How bad is it? Is it going to fall down? I saw some rotting boards..." She trailed off and waited for his professional assessment.

"Not bad," he said, surprising her. "This is a grand old place. The exterior needs some brick work, but the frame is solid steel; it's not going anywhere. I doubt a twister could take this place down. There is some dry rot and termite damage, so a lot of the floors will need to be replaced. The plumbing is a mess and needs a complete overhaul. The heating systems are also antiquated and should be replaced. You'll need a new roof—it's about to collapse—not to mention the wiring. Between the circuit overload and the dry wood, this place is a tinderbox."

"But you said it wasn't bad," she reminded him, overwhelmed by his list.

He shrugged. "I've seen worse. It needs work, but the foundation is in great shape. That means a lot in a building this old. Basically all it needs is some TLC, and it's good to go."

"How much do you think it would cost to make the renovations?"

"I'm not a contractor, and I don't give estimates," he said. By his careful tone, she wondered if she had stepped on some professional ethics.

"Off the record," she prodded. "I won't hold you to your quote. I'm looking for a ballpark figure here."

He chewed the inside of his cheek as he thought. "I'd say a million, give or take a few hundred thousand."

Lacy stared at him, speechless. A million dollars? Granted, she had a million dollars, but she hadn't planned to spend every penny on an old building she didn't even want. Fortunately, her grandfather took over the pleasantries with Mr. March. The two men exchanged small talk about what needed to be done to the building, and then Mr. March took his leave.

"What have I gotten myself into?" Lacy muttered when she and Mr. Middleton were alone.

He smiled at her, placing his arm companionably around her shoulders. "C'mon, kiddo. I'll buy you a coffee and we'll talk it over."

They went to the coffee shop where they had first connected. Lacy hadn't been there since she found out the former cashier had murdered her biological grandmother. Now there was a new cashier, one who looked oddly like Peggy, and Lacy tried to shrug off her uncomfortable feeling. Life went on. The clientele probably appreciated the continuity, even if Lacy found it creepy that nothing significant had changed. They ordered two coffees and sat across from each other at the table where, a few weeks ago, she had first blurted to him the fact that she knew he was her grandfather.

"Now tell me what you want to do with the Stakely building," her grandfather commanded.

"I guess I want to restore it to its former glory," Lacy said tentatively. When he didn't laugh, she continued. "You know, make it a marketplace and center of downtown, like you and Grandma were telling me about."

He nodded. "Sounds like a good plan."

She smiled, enjoying the fact that he didn't point out that she was a stupid kid who had no idea what she was doing. Maybe if he believed she could do something with the old place, that meant she actually could. Now it was her turn to point out the obvious.

"I have no idea what to do," she said.

He nodded once, blowing on his coffee. Since he drank his coffee at the boiling point, she thought the action was a habit more than an actual urge to cool anything. "I did a little research last night."

"You did?" He was an intelligent, thoughtful man, and she was keenly interested in any wisdom he might have to impart, especially in light of the fact that she was clueless. "What did you find out?"

"I found out the Stakely building was sort of famous when it was built. Steel-frame construction was something new at the beginning of the industrial revolution. Architects came from neighboring states to admire the design."

"It is a beautiful building," she agreed. "I've always loved it. I want to do right by it and bring it back to its former glory, but I have no idea how to afford the repairs. Even with my inheritance, it seems like a lot. And I'm not sure I want all of my inheritance to go into such a venture. How could I ever make my money back?"

"There are grants," he said. "Urban renewal grants. I think you have a compelling case, and I think you would qualify for one of the larger grants."

"How much is it?" she asked excitedly. What if a grant would take care of all the remodeling costs?

"About a hundred and fifty thousand dollars," he said.

"Oh." She sat back, dejected. That much would definitely be helpful, but it wouldn't begin to cover everything.

"That should just about cover the roof," he said. "I think you should start there. There are holes that are letting in water and warping the wood even more. Once you have the roof taken care of, you can focus on the plumbing and electrical." He paused and blew on his coffee again. "How much of my advice do you want, Lacy? I don't want to be an interfering old fool."

"You're not," she assured him. "I want to hear everything you have to say. If I don't agree with your advice, then I won't take it."

He smiled. "That's so. If I were you, I would concentrate on the third floor first. I know it's not as pretty or exciting as the open area, but it could be your bread and butter. People are always looking to rent office space. There's enough space there for an entire medical complex. Once you have stable renters who are providing income, then you can focus on renovating the first and second floors. Gradually, as you attract renters for that space, it will help fund further renovations or payback what you've already spent."

"What about the fourth floor? What do you think I should do with that?" She pictured the wide, open space.

He shrugged. "Whatever you want. It could be a warehouse, but you'll have to have the freight elevator fixed. Or it could be storage. The possibilities are unlimited."

That was both encouraging and overwhelming. What did one do with twelve thousand square feet of open space? The question reminded her that she still owned Barbara Blake's house and all her possessions, including those that had been shipped from her New York apartment. Maybe she should have them moved to the warehouse after it was clean. At the very least, it would give her the space she needed to sort the house.

"Know any good roofers?" she asked.

Her grandfather shook his head. "You'll have to have a commercial roofer; they're much different than residential. I'll ask around, but your best bet is in the city. And don't hire the first one you meet; take several bids so you can compare."

Lacy nodded, soaking up the advice like a sponge. At least she had a starting place now; she would begin at the top and redo the roof. And she would apply for a grant, the sooner the better.

The newspaper, lying on a nearby table, caught her attention. The headline screamed the news of an old case that was being reopened. Lacy grimaced at the reporter's hyperbolic writing style. She knew if the editor, Len, would allow it, the writer probably would have used exclamation points. Her enthusiasm highlighted how big the story was, causing Lacy to wonder how she had missed it.

"News broke this week that Joe Anton, arrested seven years ago for the murder of Susan Prendergast, has been slated for a retrial due to the reexamination of his case. According to his lawyer, Ed McNeil, evidence in the Prendergast case was mishandled by the arresting officer, Jason Cantor.

"The murder, which took place almost a quarter century ago, remained an open investigation for several years until new information came to light. Now that information is being called into question by Mr. Anton's attorney. The trial begins..."

Lacy stopped reading as her thoughts began to wander. No wonder Jason had been so angry with her. Instead of casting a shadow on the incompetent Detective Brenner, she had inadvertently cast a shadow over the entire sheriff's department. Jason was right; smarmy lawyers like Ed McNeil would feast on the development like vultures, plucking hapless criminals from jail in an attempt to exploit them.

"Poor Jason," Lacy muttered. She felt horrible. She hadn't meant for this to happen, but how could she have prevented it? She had no idea her article would cause trouble for him.

She bit her lip as she stared at the paper. If she had known, would she have written the article anyway? She had been incensed at the way Detective Brenner treated her grandmother, and she had wanted vengeance. But, no, she was sure that if she somehow could have foreseen the impact her article would have on the entire force, she wouldn't have written it. She had only respect for Jason's fellow officers, with the exception of Detective Brenner, of course.

"Jason will be okay," her grandfather assured her. "He's a survivor."

Lacy frowned as she was once again reminded of his earlier cryptic comment. What did he know about Jason? And, more importantly, how could she find out?

CHAPTER 4

The nice thing about being an heiress was that Lacy didn't have to work for a while. Normally she enjoyed work, but right now she was overwhelmed. The ability to make her own schedule was handy, especially now.

She wasted no time in calling as many commercial roofers as she could. Most didn't return her phone calls. Five agreed to look at the building and give her an estimate that day.

Feeling good about having accomplished her first step in renovation, she turned her focus to preparing for her evening with Tosh and his brother. Tosh called her twice to make sure she remembered, she would be there on time, and she would look good. Why was he so nervous? It was just his brother. She assured him she would be present, on time, and looking as good as possible and then ignored her phone when it jangled a third time.

Not wanting to borrow her grandmother's car a second time in a day, she walked to Tosh's house instead. He lived a couple of miles away, but the air was turning cool and the leaves were beginning to change colors, making the stroll a pleasant one.

Tosh opened the front door and stepped out onto the porch as soon as she arrived in his driveway. "I would have picked you up," he said disapprovingly.

"Nothing wrong with walking," she told him. "It does a body good."

"I don't think your body needs any improvement." The new voice spoke behind Tosh. Shoving his brother aside, he stepped out onto the porch and beamed at Lacy. Lacy stared back, speechless. Tosh hadn't warned her his brother would be so…so, well, so hot. He was as tall as Tosh, but lacking Tosh's gangly build. Instead, his form was solid and muscular, but not overly. He and Tosh shared the same sandy shade of brown hair, but that's where the similarities ended. The brother's eyes were green and sparkled with mischief as he stood on the porch and surveyed Lacy.

"This is Keegan," Tosh said lamely. "Keegan, Lacy." He waved his hand toward Lacy, as if there was a throng of women in the driveway and he needed to point out the correct one.

"Lacy," Keegan said. His eyes locked on hers and held her captive as he stepped down from the porch and stalked toward her. She wasn't sure what he would do when he reached her, but nothing prepared her for the reality. He bent and pressed his lips to hers. It was a closed-mouth kiss, but still. Lacy stared at him in shock before turning to look helplessly at Tosh.

He shrugged as if to say "That's Keegan for you."

"You taste good," Keegan told her. "Come on." He grasped her hand and tugged, leading her toward the house. She trotted helplessly behind him, shooting Tosh another questioning look as she swept up the porch beside him. He sighed and followed them inside, closing the door behind them.

Keegan led their party to the kitchen and stopped short with no warning, causing Lacy to bounce off of his back. She might have toppled to the ground if Tosh hadn't caught her. Suspiciously, she wondered if he was hovering so closely because he had been prepared for the possibility of having to rescue her from Keegan.

"Let's get to work," Keegan said. He began zooming around the kitchen, opening cupboards and pulling out items.

When Lacy could take it no longer, she finally turned to ask Tosh her questions. "What is he doing?" she asked in a stage whisper.

"He's cooking. Didn't I mention that Keegan is a gourmet chef?" he whispered.

"No, you didn't mention anything about him," she said, elbowing him lightly in the stomach.

He draped his arm around her shoulders and gave them a squeeze. "Hmm, must have slipped my mind."

"Is that what he does for a living?"

Tosh shook his head. "No, he's a foreman for a construction company."

She frowned. Tosh's family was wealthy. Why did Keegan work construction? "Your family's construction company?" she guessed.

Tosh nodded. "Our other brother handles the business end of things with our dad. Keegan prefers to take a more hands-on role. He actually works construction, doing the heavy lifting and pounding of nails, things like that."

"Do you think he might look at the Stakely building and give me some pointers?" she whispered.

Keegan paused in his preparations to look at them. "You know I can hear you," he said.

Lacy smiled sheepishly and he beamed at her. "The answer to your question is yes, I would love to look at your building. What building?"

She explained to him how she had bought the Stakely building.

"Cool." He resumed his preparations, ignoring her and Tosh once again.

"How did it go today with the inspector?" Tosh asked. He kept his arm around her, his fingers twirling distractedly in her hair. To Keegan, they must have looked like a couple. Lacy was once again suspicious. Tosh was an affectionate person, but was his display for Keegan's sake?

"Okay I guess." She told him about the meeting, as well as her grandfather's suggestions for the renovation. She didn't think Keegan was paying any attention to them, but then he spoke up.

"You should go green. You can get more grant money, and it might help you in the long run."

"Go green?" she asked.

He nodded. "Solar panels, that type of thing. Your up front cost will be greater, but the return might be worth it, especially if the building costs a lot to operate, which it undoubtedly does. Our buildings are big into green development now. I'll give you some pointers when I look at the building."

"Thanks, Keegan," she said sincerely. Help was springing up from all sources, and Lacy felt deeply grateful.

He smiled at her again while he chopped a pepper and tossed it in a bowl. Something about the scene caused her mind to flash to Jason and the times he had cooked for her. Her heart gave a painful twist as a sudden wave of longing washed over her. She hated that he was angry at her, and she hated that her story was causing him problems. But what could she do?

"You're sad," Tosh said. Despite the fact that he sometimes spoke without thinking, he was a warm, caring person, sensitive to the moods of those around him.

"I have a lot on my mind," she hedged. Lacy didn't want to spout her problems in front of Keegan, but she also didn't want to unload on Tosh about Jason. The two didn't care for each other, and she was careful not to talk about one to the other.

Keegan looked up with another mischievous smile. "If you two want to go in the other room for some alone time, I won't be offended."

Lacy started to protest, but Tosh took her hand and tugged her toward his living room. "Thanks," he called to his brother.

"Tosh," she whispered when they were alone. "He thinks we're coming in here to make out."

"Then we shouldn't disappoint him," Tosh replied, drawing her close and putting his arms around her.

She gave his chest a light shove. "Be serious."

He let her go and rolled his eyes. "Being friends with you is like taking a battering ram to my ego sometimes. It might surprise you to know some women do find me attractive."

"I find you attractive," she blurted, anxious to make amends so no more of her friends would be angry with her. The universe might implode if Tosh and Jason both stopped speaking to her. At least, her universe would implode.

"Really?" Tosh drawled. "Tell me more."

She laughed and shook her head. "Meeting your brother has made me more curious about your family. Are they all like you two?" Tosh and Keegan were irrepressible. How could one family produce more than two such characters?

"No," Tosh said. "Keegan and I are the shy ones."

Lacy laughed, and it felt good. Tosh smiled. "You have the best laugh, Lacy." He drew her close again, but this time it was for a friendly hug. She rested her head on his chest and enjoyed the comforting warmth of his embrace.

"This is more like it," Keegan said approvingly as he arrived unannounced in the room. "Supper is ready."

Lacy poked Tosh in the side. "Tell him the truth about us," she whispered.

He sighed as he led the way back into the kitchen. "Keegan, Lacy and I aren't actually dating," he said. "Technically. I mean, we spend almost all our time together, go out every weekend, and have kissed, but…"

"We're not dating," Lacy cut in with an annoyed glance in Tosh's direction. "We're friends, very good friends."

"Really?" Keegan asked. He set down the dish he was holding and leaned toward her. "So you're available then?"

"No," she said. "I mean, I'm physically available, but emotionally…" She trailed off, not wanting to get into her life's history with this stranger, even though he was staring at her with the same concerned look Tosh often gave her. The compassion gene must run strong in their family. "Tosh and I have a lot of fun together," she said. "But I'm not ready for anything more with anyone right now."

"Hmm," Keegan said, eyeing her thoughtfully. "We need to figure out a way to get you over the hump and back on your feet again."

"Exactly," Tosh agreed. "That's what I've been trying to tell her. She needs to date someone loving, caring, and loyal to prove to her that all guys aren't jerks." Lacy knew he considered himself to be that guy.

"Nah," Keegan said. "She needs to have a wild fling where she's the one in control. Then she can walk away and know she has her esteem still intact."

Tosh shook his head. Lacy wondered if he, too, was thinking of Jason just then. "No way. Lacy's not like that. She's not a fling type person."

"And that's why it's perfect," Keegan said. "She should break out of the mold and do something different."

The brothers bickered for a couple of minutes until Lacy finally interrupted. "Uh, guys, I'm right here. You're talking about me like I'm not in the room."

"That's because we're trying to figure out what's best for you, Lacy," Keegan assured her. "Enjoy your food until we get your life figured out. It should only take another minute or two." He smiled at her and winked. "Speaking of your life, my brother is being a real drag and dumping me off to fend for myself tomorrow. Why don't we go see your building?"

"That would be perfect," Lacy enthused. "The roofers are supposed to give me their estimates tomorrow. Maybe you can help me choose one."

"Sounds good," Keegan said. "Too bad we don't live closer, or our company could do it."

"Do you take on little projects like mine?" she asked. When she pictured Tosh's family's company holdings, she imagined them doing things on a grand scale, like building skyscrapers.

"Not usually, but for a friend we might make an exception." He gave her another wink, moved closer, and rested his arm on the back of her chair as he launched into another narrative about construction. It wasn't until Lacy was lying in her bed that night going to sleep that she realized Tosh hadn't said another word the rest of the evening, not even a goodbye when she left his house.

CHAPTER 5

The next morning, Lacy ran into a problem. Randy Stone, the first roofing contractor to call her, told her that he couldn't do the estimate for the Stakely building because someone had put a stop-work order on her property.

She sat up so abruptly she almost fell out of bed. "What? How is that possible? I've owned it exactly two days."

"I did some checking," he said sympathetically. "The order was placed by Ed McNeil. He was the previous property manager, and he says you owe him money. I've heard that he does this type of thing a lot because he figures people will pay him off rather than go through the hassle of trying to fight him. The good news is that I think he's performed some legal cartwheels to make this thing stick. If you found another lawyer, you could probably have it undone."

"He thought wrong this time because I am going to fight him," she said, so furious she was practically shaking with anger. "I'm not going to find another lawyer; I'm going to track him down and make him remove it myself." As soon as Ed McNeil handed over her inheritance, she promptly transferred her holdings to another law firm. She had paid him for the work he did on her behalf, as well as the work he did for her grandmother. His fees had been exorbitant, but it had been worth it to get her grandmother out of jail so promptly. Lacy was sure, however, that she owed him nothing else.

She was glad for the procrastination that had prevented her from erasing his number from her phone. Now with the touch of a button she could gain verbal retribution without ever getting out of bed.

"Mr. McNeil's office," an official-sounding voice answered. Lacy was momentarily puzzled before remembering that Mr. McNeil's secretary had been out sick during Lacy's interaction with the man.

"May I speak with Mr. McNeil, please?" She tried to be polite; no need to take out her frustration on his hapless secretary.

"Whom may I tell him is calling?"

"Lacy Steele."

"He's out."

Lacy pulled the phone away from her ear and looked at it, trying to determine if she had imagined the abrupt change in tone. "May I leave a message?"

"I'll tell him you called," the secretary replied, and then the phone slammed hard in Lacy's ear.

"What was that about?" Lacy muttered. Determined to try again later, she set the phone aside and burrowed out of her covers. It was early, but any future chance of sleep was over.

Jason popped into her head while she was showering, which was unfortunate timing. After she was thoroughly dressed and fed, she called him and reached his voicemail.

"It's Lacy. I just wanted to say that..." She broke off, realizing she had no idea what to say. After a few seconds of thought, she decided to be honest. "I don't like it when things are like this between us. I'm sorry I caused you so much trouble, and I'm here if you need me."

She ended the call and stared at the phone, wishing there was more she could do or say to make amends. Then again, she didn't want him to think she was chasing him. She had made a move toward reconciliation; now the ball was in his court.

Keegan had a rental car and he had volunteered to drive to the Stakely building, so after Lacy was finished getting ready, she had nothing to do but wait for him to arrive. She decided to call Tosh while she was waiting, but there was no answer and she got his voice-mail, too.

"Tosh, I was just seeing if you're coming with us today. You're welcome to. I wasn't sure if I made that clear last night." She bit her lip, feeling like she should add more, but she didn't know what. "If you don't come with us today, I hope we can talk tonight." She paused again, trying to figure out why she felt the urge to apologize to Tosh, too. "Bye," she said at last. She hadn't done anything to Tosh, had she? There was nothing she could think of, but she still had the uneasy feeling he was upset with her.

There wasn't much time to brood, however, because almost as soon as she ended the call, Keegan was knocking on her door.

"Hey, pretty lady," he said as soon as she answered. Then he bent and kissed her cheek.

"Hey," she said. She felt comfortable with him, but she didn't want to give him the wrong idea, so she made no move to return the kiss.

"Ready?" he asked.

In answer, she smiled, nodded, and followed him to his car. "Thanks for picking me up," she said.

"Tosh tells me you don't have a car," he said.

She shrugged. Previously she hadn't bought a car because she hadn't been able to afford one. But now that she could afford one, she wasn't sure she needed one. At least not yet, anyway. Here she could walk almost anywhere she needed to go, and she liked that.

Keegan must have read a lot into her shrug because he laughed. "You're a throwback, Lacy. Very retro."

Since she had no idea what that meant, she let it go.

The drive downtown took less than two minutes, so there wasn't much time for conversation. But when he parked the car and looked up at the building, he whistled. "You bought this? That is so awesome, Lacy, I love it."

They sat in the car for a full minute as Keegan peered through the windshield, taking in the building from top to bottom. As he studied the building, Lacy studied him. She couldn't quite figure him out. On the surface of things, he seemed sweet and innocent, handsome and happy go lucky. But Lacy sensed there was something more going on behind the façade. Keegan was holding something back.

She gave herself a mental shake. Of course he was holding back; they were strangers. Just because they had Tosh in common didn't make them instant best friends. Why would he open up to her about his life when he didn't know her from Eve? Still, she felt his inner conflict palpably, either because it was obvious or because she was attuned to him in the same mysterious way she was attuned to Tosh. As she watched his smile slowly fade and his eyes become troubled, she thought maybe it was the former. But before she could ask him if he was okay, he pasted his perfect smile back in place and opened his door.

"Let's take a look inside," he said, sounding once again like a kid who was about to receive a new toy.

His enthusiasm was catching, and she found herself laughing as she trotted behind him, half sprinting to reach the entrance. As soon as she unlocked the door, he clasped her hand and led her into the building before stopping short in the entryway.

"Oh, wow," he said, and by his serious expression she wasn't sure if he meant it in a good way or a bad way. Then he turned his beaming smile on her and removed all doubt. "This is awesome." He drew out each word. "Show me everything," he commanded.

And she did. They spent the next hour going over every detail of the place. Keegan spent an inordinate amount of time looking at the architectural details and the roof. Lacy hovered near the door during that part, not being a huge fan of heights. Keegan, however, was fearless, walking to the edge and leaning far over in a move that left Lacy breathless. Her natural instinct was to caution him, but she wasn't his mother, and he was a professional contractor.

"So what do you think?" she asked when he finally—thankfully—stopped hanging over the edge of the roof.

"I think my first instinct was right; you should go green. But I don't just mean going solar—I mean a living roof up here."

"Living roof?" she repeated, only vaguely guessing at what that might mean.

He nodded. "This part here," he pointed to half the roof, "would be perfect for a living roof. You could put the solar panels over there." He paused to point again. "And then this area would be your living space."

"Living space?" she repeated dumbly.

"Living space," he said. "Don't tell me you're not planning to live here when it's done, Lacy. You have the most amazing loft on the fourth floor and with this roof, well, it's spectacular."

"No, I'm not planning to live here," Lacy said. "I'm going to..." She broke off as she once again realized she had no idea what she was going to do. "In any case, I'm not going to live here."

"Why not?" Keegan asked.

"It's so...big," she said.

"Most people want space."

"Not by myself," she said, uncomfortable at revealing too much to a near stranger. How could she tell him she couldn't imagine living anywhere so vast? The cavernous space would no doubt echo her loneliness.

Keegan grinned. "So marry my brother and fill it with babies."

"Keegan," she said, blushing faintly at the mention of babies.

"What?" he asked with mock innocence. "Can't blame a guy for wanting to see his brother happy. Tosh likes you, Lacy, and that's saying something. And you're better than his usual type of girl. Don't tell him I said so, but he has lousy taste in women. You're a keeper. And you'd make a good mom."

Lacy laughed, a small, uncomfortable sound that did nothing to ease her pressing anxiety. "You've come to this conclusion after twelve hours of knowing me?"

"I have good instincts," Keegan said.

Lacy shook her head, rolling her eyes, all the while wondering about Tosh's other women. He had never mentioned anyone he'd dated. "What about you? When are you going to settle down and have babies?"

For the briefest of seconds, his happy smile fled. "That remains to be seen," he said seriously. Then he stepped forward and clasped her hand again, pulling her back inside the building.

"So when are you going to get started on this?" Keegan asked as soon as they were safely on the ground and standing by his car.

"As soon as I can get some estimates, but I can't get any estimates until Ed McNeil takes the stop-work order off this place." Leave it to Ed McNeil to figure out a way around the system. "Can you drop me by his office?"

"You want me to come in and have a little talk with him?"

By the way he frowned as he popped his knuckles, she wasn't sure if he meant talk or *talk*. The sudden vision of Keegan getting arrested for beating up Ed McNeil was enough to make her refuse his offer.

"No, thanks, I can handle this myself." She tried to sound more confident than she felt. Ed McNeil was smarmy and smooth. He was a weasel who could seemingly get away with murder in this town. What chance did she have against him when he apparently knew every trick in the book?

She needn't have worried, though. As soon as she reached his office, she realized there was no getting around his giant roadblock of a secretary, Pearl. Lacy wondered if there was some mistake. Surely the large woman sitting behind the desk couldn't be named something as delicate as Pearl, but that's what her nameplate read.

When Lacy cleared her throat, Pearl looked up with a welcoming smile that soon froze and hardened. How was it possible that she recognized Lacy when the two had never met?

"Mr. McNeil's not in, Miss Steele," Pearl said with no friendly preamble.

"Where can I find him?" Lacy said, trying not to be intimidated by the woman's fierce expression, booming voice, and large size.

"He's in court today, which means he's off limits to you." She returned her attention to her desk, effectively dismissing Lacy.

"Excuse me, Miss, uh, Pearl," Lacy paused, suddenly wondering if Pearl was her first name or last name. It was the only one listed on her nameplate. "Why do you seem so hostile to me when we've never met?"

Pearl looked up then, her eyes flashing fire. "I don't like women who take advantage of Mr. McNeil's kindness."

Lacy wasn't sure what was most troubling about that statement, the fact that she thought Lacy had taken advantage or the fact that she thought Mr. McNeil was kind.

"What are you talking about?" she asked.

Pearl narrowed her eyes. Lacy couldn't help but feel like a mouse standing in front of a python. "Mr. McNeil helped your grandmother out of a very tight situation, and then you left him high and dry without paying your bills. Now that he's trying to collect on the debt due him, you're about to make a fuss and say it isn't so. Don't try to deny it; I can tell your type."

Lacy's jaw dropped. The woman was all but shaking with rage. Was she mental? The answer to that was obvious. "I did pay Mr. McNeil."

"I have no record of your payment. If you'd like to pay today, I can make copies of your receipts."

"But *I* have record of my payment. He didn't give me a receipt, but I have my own financial records. I certainly didn't pay in cash." Lacy had purposely created a paper trail, not trusting Ed McNeil, especially not when he had put off giving her a receipt by saying his secretary handled all the paperwork and he didn't know how.

"Those things can be faked, of course," Pearl said, her obstinate tone telling Lacy she didn't believe a word. "Mr. McNeil works very hard, and it's people like you who take advantage of his good nature that make this job hard."

There was a part of Lacy that wanted to keep arguing with her, but if she did, she had a feeling she would wind up as insane as Pearl McCrazypants. Instead, she simply swallowed her retort and left the office, intending to track down Ed McNeil and get to the bottom of it with him.

He's good, Lacy thought. *Hiring someone crazy whose devotion to him knows no bounds. Is there anything Ed McNeil* won't *do? How low could he go?*

She had no idea that when she reached the courthouse, she would get an answer to that question.

CHAPTER 6

There were two courtrooms within the courthouse—one for municipal court, and one for the Court of Common Pleas. Since Ed McNeil usually handled high profile defense cases (or at least high profile in their small town), it was a safe bet that he was in felony court. Lacy turned toward the Court of Common Pleas and opened the door, slipping quietly inside.

She almost gave herself away, however, when she realized the person on the stand was Jason. With a stifled yelp of surprise, she took her seat, instinctively positioning herself behind the person in front of her so she couldn't be seen. Even though she hadn't yet heard a word, she somehow knew Jason wouldn't want her to hear what was about to take place. Lacy thought the examination had just begun. There was a sense of anticipation and settling in as everyone shuffled around and leaned forward intently.

"Officer Cantor, you were the arresting officer in this case, were you not?" Ed McNeil asked. The way he paced regally back and forth in front of Jason with his head down and hands clasped behind his back reminded Lacy of Foghorn Leghorn from the old cartoons.

"I was," Jason replied. His voice was tense, the way it was when he was trying to keep a tight leash on his temper.

Calm down, Jason, she silently pled, knowing it wouldn't do him any favors if he lost it with Ed McNeil, especially because that was probably exactly what the unctuous lawyer wanted.

"On the night in question seven years ago, how did you find the defendant when you went to arrest him?" Ed McNeil paused mid-pace and turned to the defense table where a pathetic-looking man sat hunched behind the desk, his prison-issued orange uniform dwarfing his small frame. His hair was white and thinning. Lacy couldn't see his expression, but she wondered if it was as dejected as the rest of his posture.

"I found him high on a substance later determined to be heroin," Jason said.

"And what was his reaction to you? Was he violent? Did he resist arrest?"

"No," Jason said. "He was confused, but he didn't put up a struggle. I read him his rights, cuffed him, and put him in the back of my cruiser."

"What led to Mr. Anton's arrest that night, Officer?" Ed McNeil asked.

Lacy's hand clenched into a fist. She felt he was leading somewhere, but she didn't know where.

"I wasn't part of the investigative process until the very end," Jason said. "I stumbled across an inconsistency in his statement and his alibi. From there we were able to determine that Mr. Anton's alibi had been false. Not only that, but he and the victim had recently had an argument, providing him with motive. That, combined with the fact that the defendant had been a known drug user during the time of the murder was enough evidence to make the arrest. More information came to light at trial, and it was enough to convict him."

"So because my client used drugs and had argued with the victim some thirteen years before his arrest, he was automatically a prime suspect. Why after thirteen years was he a suspect again, officer?"

Jason took a breath, fighting an exasperated sigh. "The case had been open for years, the file in the patrol room for anyone to look at. I took an interest in it when I joined the force and began pursuing the angles again. That's when I ran across the inconsistencies with Mr. Anton."

"So, just to clarify, you—a rookie, brand new to the force and still wet behind the ears—singlehandedly solved a case that your fellow officers had been unable to solve for thirteen years."

"No, I did nothing singlehandedly. I consulted with the detectives and built upon the work that had already been done. If my superiors and the prosecutor hadn't agreed with my conclusion, they wouldn't have worked so hard to get the warrant. And then a jury of his peers convicted him based on that same evidence."

"Thank you for that summation, Officer Cantor," Ed McNeil said, his tone sarcastic. "How long have you been on the force now?"

"Seven years," Jason said tightly.

"In that time, how many complaints have been lodged against you?"

"It would be unnatural if the people I arrested didn't complain. But no complaint has ever stuck, none has ever required an official investigation," Jason said.

"How many?" Ed McNeil pressed.

"Three," Jason said through gritted teeth. "But as I said…"

"So three citizens have complained about your rough treatment and mishandling of their cases, and your superiors have never investigated their golden boy," Ed McNeil said.

"Objection," the prosecutor said, rising to his feet. "Your honor, Officer Cantor is an exemplary employee whose record speaks for itself."

"I withdraw my statement," Ed McNeil said before the judge could make a decision. He held up his hands in surrender as if to imply he meant no offense. "Since opposing counsel mentioned it, let's talk a little about your record, Officer. You grew up in this town, is that correct?"

"That's correct," Jason said. Lacy could practically feel the tension radiating off him.

"Your grades were excellent. You were the salutatorian, received the perfect attendance award every year, and never got in trouble. You were also the quarterback for our esteemed football team, isn't that correct, Officer?"

"Yes," Jason said. For some reason, the recap of his life was making him tenser and angrier, as if he sensed where it was leading.

"Forgive me for asking, Officer, but why would someone who showed so much promise stay home and become a small-town cop?"

Lacy held her breath; she had asked herself this same question many times. Jason also took a breath and let it out slowly before answering. "This is my home, and I've always wanted to be a cop, to make a difference."

"Let's be honest, Officer. There's a reason you're so interested in the law, isn't there?" Before Jason answered, he continued, pounding out the words like an accusation. "In fact, your family has a long history with our police department. I hold in my hand at least fifty calls to your house on domestic complaints varying from arguing to downright abuse. Isn't that so, Officer?"

"Objection," the prosecutor said, rising to his feet in outrage. "Your honor, I don't see what any of this has to do with…"

But Ed McNeil talked overtop of him, pressing his point in a near shout. "Your father beating your mother, beating you, screaming at the neighbors, your mother screaming at him, screaming at you. Certainly that kind of childhood can't help but leave scars, can it?"

The judge banged his gavel, trying in vain to silence Ed McNeil. "That's enough, Ed," the judge said, clearly angry. "That kind of stuff won't fly in my courtroom, and you know it. The officer's childhood has nothing to do with the case in question today, and the jury is advised to disregard anything that was just said in the last few minutes." He narrowed his eyes, jabbing his gavel in Ed McNeil's direction. "One more trick like that, and I'll declare a mistrial. You understand me, Ed?"

Ed McNeil nodded, hanging his head as if sorry for his behavior. When he turned to head back to his table, the person in front of Lacy shifted to the right, allowing her a direct line to Jason's sight. Jason chose that moment look straight ahead. Their eyes locked and held until the judge spoke.

"You're dismissed, Officer, with the court's apologies."

Finally, agonizingly, Jason tore his gaze from Lacy and walked down from the stand. Lacy was glad there were a few formalities before court adjourned so she could try and compose her scattered thoughts.

Growing up, Jason had always been one of the beautiful people whose life had seemed perfect. But behind the fair façade, he was hiding a dirty secret. His home life had been chaotic at the least and abusive at the worst. As the shocking information began to sink in, the pieces started to click together. No wonder Jason had thrown himself into school. No wonder he was so dedicated to being a cop. No wonder he was such a neat freak. It didn't take a professional psychologist to see that he was trying to order his world, to make sense of the chaos, and right the wrongs from his past.

Though she had no idea what to say to him, she had to talk to him. But when she scanned the courtroom, he was nowhere in sight. Had he slipped out when she hadn't been watching? Granted, she had been zoned out for the last few minutes now. In fact, as she came to, she realized with a start that court had been adjourned and all the key players were absent, including Ed McNeil, the person she had come to see.

Lacy stood, gathered her purse, and rushed into the hallway. Ed McNeil stood in the circle of three reporters. Lacy could tell they were reporters because of the recording devices they held in front of Ed McNeil's face. She was surprised by the attention this case was receiving. Their town was small and far from a large news source. With chagrin, she realized it was probably her article that had sparked an interest in the case. She bit back a groan; Jason would never forgive her for this.

When the lawyer was at last finished hamming it up for the cameras, Lacy advanced on him, but he held up a hand to ward her off.

"Not now, Lacy. I'm very busy."

"I need to talk to you," she said, jogging to keep pace with him as he strutted down the corridor.

"I don't have time right now. I have another meeting."

"When is a good time? I can't seem to get a straight answer from your Attila the Hun secretary, and this concerns a great deal of money."

He paused. If there was one thing Ed McNeil appreciated, it was the almighty dollar. Lacy was momentarily distracted by the sight of his garish pinky ring, glittering in the fluorescent lights as he ran his hands through his greasy hair. "I'll be in my office tomorrow morning and my secretary has a dentist appointment. Stop by then, but keep it short. I'm very busy." With that he turned and continued his walk toward the exit while Lacy scowled at his back. Out of the corner of her eye, she saw the flash of a dark uniform. Hoping it was Jason, she changed direction and hurried around the corner, but it was too late. If it was him, he had gone. Figuring out what to say to him would have to wait until she could find him. She tried not to feel relieved that she wouldn't have to think up something to say. What was there to say?

Sorry you had a horrific childhood. Sorry I complain about all my petty problems when you have real issues to deal with. Sorry I thought your life was perfect when it's much worse than mine has ever been. Maybe she shouldn't say a word. Maybe she should just hug him.

She gave a humorless chuckle as she tried to imagine hugging Jason in his current mood. She would have better luck hugging a hungry grizzly. Maybe she should give him some time to cool off; she certainly wouldn't want to be the recipient of his now-raging temper.

CHAPTER 7

By the time Lacy left the courthouse, she had come to her senses and overcome her fear of confronting Jason. He was her friend and, bad mood or not, he had to be hurting over such a public and humiliating airing of his family's dirty laundry. She had to see him, had to let him know that he wasn't alone. She pulled out her phone and called him, gritting her teeth in impatience when she once again reached his voicemail.

"I'm starting to feel like your stalker," she said. "For your information, I am not the woman who calls and leaves fifty messages on a guy's voicemail, but I get the sense you're dodging me, and I don't like that. I've already apologized, but I'll do it again. I'm sorry I brought this whole mess about. It wasn't my intention, and I hope you know that. I go off a little half-cocked when I'm angry. No big surprise there." She paused. "Jason, I'm sorry. And I want you to know that the stuff from court…it's not…relevant to…who you are…to our…friendship." She sighed again. "I'm making a mess out of this. I hate voicemail," she said, and then the machine cut her off, ending her message most awkwardly. With a huff of frustration, she glared at her phone. Resisting the urge to toss it against the nearest wall, she instead shoved it forcefully in her pocket. Tightening her grip on her purse, she jogged down the stairs.

She had only gone a few steps when her phone rang. She was so startled to hear Jason's tone that she tripped on the last step, barely catching herself on the metal banister in time to avoid a disastrous fall.

"Hello," she said, her voice breathless as she tried to calm the rapid beating of her heart.

"Geez, are you okay?" Jason asked.

She rolled her eyes. Leave it to him to be concerned about her at a time like this. "I fell down the stairs a little. I'm fine."

He chuckled and tried to turn it into a cough. "Only you, Red, you know that?"

"Lots of people fall down the stairs, Jason," she said.

"If you say so," he said. There was an awkward pause.

"So," Lacy started, but Jason cut her off.

"Lacy, I really don't want to talk about it."

"I was simply going to ask who you thought was going to win the Super Bowl this year. I hear the Cardinals have an excellent shot, which is good because I've always liked St. Louis."

"The St. Louis Cardinals are a baseball team. I think maybe you mean the Arizona Cardinals."

"I don't think so because I don't really care for Arizona. Too dry."

"Either you're really good at offering a distraction, or you're really bad at understanding sports," Jason said.

"Maybe it's a combination," Lacy said. There was another pause, but it was more comfortable this time. "I don't like how we left things the other night," she added, trying to hash out at least one of the issues between them.

"Neither do I," Jason said. "You drive me crazy, though, Lacy. You really, really do."

"One 'really' would have been plenty, Jason," she said.

"I don't think so, Red. In fact, sometimes I think there aren't enough adjectives in the world to describe what you do to me." This time when he paused, tension practically sizzled the line between them. "I should probably go," he said at last.

She wanted to ask where he was going to go, what he was going to do, how he was feeling. But she had no right to ask any of those things. Or maybe she did, but she was afraid to, afraid to get too close to him, to cross the fine line they had been dancing for the last few weeks.

"Jason," she began, feeling her way uncertainly. "You know I'm here, right? If you want to talk or…" she broke off, not knowing how to continue.

"It's the 'or' that intrigues me and keeps me up at night, Red," Jason said. She could tell he was smiling, and she smiled in return.

"For the record, Ed McNeil deserves to be horsewhipped for what he did to you, and I plan to tell him the next time I see him," she added, feeling angry all over again.

"He deserves more than a whipping," Jason said, his tone turning gritty and hard. "He deserves to be shot."

"Well, I suppose you would feel that way," Lacy said, trying to overlook the disconcerting imagery the words had caused.

"It's not the way I feel; it's a fact. He's a bottom feeder who deserves what's coming to him."

"Jason, you don't really mean that," Lacy said softly.

Jason pulled in a breath, held it, and let it out slowly. "No, I don't really mean that. Still, though, he's not on my list of favorite people."

"I bet there are a lot of people who will be crossing him off their Christmas card lists this year," Lacy said, frowning.

Jason laughed. "Ah, Lacy, don't let this go to your head, but your innocent mind and Miss Priss attitude are good for me."

"Miss Priss?" Lacy repeated, outraged.

"Forget it. Let's say goodbye now before the warm fuzzies go away and we start fighting again. Later, Red."

Before she could reply, he hung up. Almost as soon as she closed her phone, it rang again. This time it was another roofer, telling her he couldn't do the promised estimate until the stop-work order was removed.

"I'll take care of it tomorrow," she assured him. "Stupid Ed McNeil," she yelled as she tucked the phone back in her pocket, startling the man walking beside her so that he jumped and moved away from her.

Head down in embarrassment now, she started walking, and then her phone rang again. This time she smiled when she heard the tone, knowing it was Tosh.

"Hey," she said. "Took you long enough to call me back."

"I was supposed to call you back?" Keegan said.

"Are you using Tosh's phone?"

"How else was I supposed to get your number? Is it okay that I called?"

"Of course," she said. "I just thought it was Tosh. How is he?" *Why hasn't he returned my call?*

"Stuffy and boring. He's ditching me tonight for some church thing."

"It's Wednesday night; I think that's just church," she said.

"You Protestants and your overconsumption of church. What's the big deal about going once a week? We Catholics had the system perfected until Martin Luther came along and ruined it."

"You're arguing with the wrong protestant," she told him. "I'm not a card-carrying member of anywhere."

"You don't go to Tosh's church?" he asked, surprised.

"Sure I do. I wouldn't want to hurt Tosh's feelings. But I'm sort of on the fringe of things. The real power players are my grandmother's group of friends. I call them the blue-hair mafia. You don't want to mess with them."

"Sounds scary," Keegan said. "I hope Tosh is safe here."

"Tosh knows how to handle the geriatric set," Lacy assured him. "He has special skills."

Keegan laughed. "You mean he's a suck-up. I'm going to tell him you said that."

"Don't give him more reason to be upset with me," Lacy said, only half joking. Why did it feel like Tosh was now dodging her?

"So, are you free tonight?" Keegan pressed.

"Sure, I guess. What did you have in mind?"

"It's a surprise. I'll pick you up at six." With that, he hung up.

"Doesn't anyone say goodbye anymore?" she asked, causing yet another passerby to look at her in alarm. "I have got to stop talking to myself," she muttered, putting her head down once again and heading to her car before remembering she didn't have one.

It's been a busy day, and you're overwhelmed, she reassured herself. *You're not actually crazy; senility won't settle in until much later in life.* With that comforting thought in mind, she began the long walk home.

CHAPTER 8

When Lacy arrived home and saw her grandparents sitting close together on the couch, their heads almost touching as her grandfather's arm rested on her grandmother's shoulders, Lacy remembered what Tosh had said. Was it time to move out of her grandmother's house? The thought of being on her own was nearly as painful as the thought that her grandparents might resent her presence.

They turned to her with welcoming smiles, but she felt paranoid now, as if she were intruding on their alone time. "I'm going out tonight," she proclaimed, lest they get the idea that she was going to hang out in the living room and badger them.

"All right, dear," her grandmother, ever the loving encourager, said with a smile. "That sounds nice. Which one are you seeing tonight?"

Lacy winced. Why did she have to make it sound like Lacy had a string of beaux, just waiting for her to choose them? "I'm going out with Tosh's brother, Keegan. He's visiting from Chicago."

"How nice," Lucinda said with a vague smile. Lacy knew that if push came to shove, Tosh would be her grandmother's choice for her. He was, after all, her pastor. What grandmother didn't dream of seeing her granddaughter married to a nice, wholesome pastor?

Though the "wholesome" image didn't always fit Tosh. He was a bit of a rogue cleric, in Lacy's opinion.

"What do we know about this Keegan boy?" her grandfather asked, his eyes narrowed thoughtfully as he studied Lacy.

Lacy smiled. "He's very nice. He runs his family's construction company, and he looked at the Stakely building for me today. He thinks we should use solar panels and make part of the roof a garden."

"That's actually a good idea," Mr. Middleton admitted begrudgingly.

"You'll like him," Lacy assured him.

"I'm sure we will," Lucinda said. "After all, he's Pastor Underwood's brother."

Mr. Middleton smiled at her in the same amused way that Tosh and Jason often smiled at Lacy. "Don't you know when one kid goes good in a family, the other usually goes bad, Lucy?" he asked, his tone teasing.

Lacy didn't mention that Tosh was probably the bad one in this scenario. He hadn't told her exactly what was in his wild past before he sewed his oats, but she guessed it was fairly epic.

"Oh, Tom, I'm sure he's a nice young man, or Lacy wouldn't have anything to do with him," Lucinda assured him, patting his arm.

"That's so," Mr. Middleton agreed. "Our Lacy's sensible." They turned beaming smiles of approval on Lacy who smiled awkwardly at being caught in the sudden spotlight. What did people do when they weren't able to bask in their grandparents' love? Her thoughts turned to Jason and something he had once said to her. *Not all of us have grandparents standing by, waiting to pick up the pieces of our shattered lives.* Was he really all alone in the world?

"Lacy, are you okay, dear?" her grandmother asked.

Lacy snapped back to attention and gave her grandparents an unconvincing smile. "Long day." She edged farther into the room and sank into the chair across from the couch. "I went to Jason's trial today. It was a smear campaign. Ed McNeil brought up a lot of garbage from his past." Her eyes met those of her grandfather as silent communication passed between them. This was the baggage he had been referring to from Jason's past, the reason he was a survivor.

Her grandmother, who believed all the world's ills could be solved with sugar, stood and bustled to the kitchen to retrieve a treat for Lacy. Or maybe she simply sensed that Lacy wanted a moment alone with her grandfather.

"Was it as bad as Ed McNeil made it sound?" Lacy asked.

Mr. Middleton sat back with a weary sigh. "It was probably worse. I can't believe he brought all that up. That man is a devil."

For the first time, Lacy let herself feel all that she had been holding back. Her eyes filled with tears. "I wish I didn't know. I wish I could go back to being ignorant, to thinking Jason's life was perfect."

"No one's life is perfect, Lacy. Our trials and tribulations shape us into who we are; it's what shape you turn into that counts, and I think Jason's turned out pretty well. Don't you?"

"Yes," Lacy said, nodding as she sniffled. "He's such a hard-working perfectionist. And he's so…" she trailed off, realizing the direction of her thoughts and how they must sound to her grandfather. "Well, he's a good guy," she finished lamely.

"I think so, too," her grandfather agreed with a benevolent smile. His eyes glazed as he stared blankly at the television, remembering. "It was hard back then, knowing what he was going through and seeing how hard he worked to keep it hidden from his friends. There are some kids you don't forget for one reason or another. Jason was one of those. I'm glad to see his life is on track." He snapped back into focus and looked at Lacy. "I'm glad he has you."

"I'm not sure he does," Lacy admitted. "Sometimes it seems like we're on our way to becoming good friends, and sometimes we can't stop fighting for two minutes."

Mr. Middleton's only reply was a sort of knowing smile that made Lacy turn away to avoid blushing.

"Peanut butter cookies," Lucinda announced by way of greeting as she entered the room. She shoved a small plate in Lacy's hands and stepped back.

"Thanks, Grandma," Lacy said. She picked up one of the cookies, only intending to take a polite bite so as not to hurt her grandmother's feelings, but as her thoughts swirled, she kept picking at the cookies until she had unwittingly eaten the entire plate. *Great*, she thought. *I can practically hear myself getting fatter.* "I think I'll go for a run before Keegan gets here." She stood, carrying her plate into the kitchen on her way to her room.

The weather was somewhere between crisp and warm with the spicy scent of falling leaves permeating the air. It was only September, but the leaves seemed to be dropping earlier this year. Or maybe it was just Lacy projecting her gloomy mood on the rest of the world. At least now she wasn't drenched in sweat every time she went for a jog, however. Spring and fall were the only brief windows of time where running was even slightly tolerable. Then came summer and winter where she was either freezing or melting, adding to her misery as she pounded the pavement.

As she suited up and began to jog, Lacy tried, really tried, to let her mind go and allow the endorphins to take over. Other people found running to be a stress reliever. Why shouldn't she? But as she took each step, all she could think was how much her lungs burned, how the cookies now sat like lead in her stomach, how she wanted more cookies as soon as she arrived home, how she must look to passersby in her mismatched spandex that did nothing to stop her from jiggling in all the wrong places. And no matter how hard she tried, she could never seem to find a smooth stride. Instead she ran with a herky-jerky motion as if she were an injured soldier trying to flee from a live grenade. One leg always seemed to drag a half step behind the other, forcing her stomach to twist at an unnatural angle as she tried to bring it even again.

By the time she arrived home, she was exhausted, gross, and ready for another shower. She had just finished applying her mascara when Keegan knocked on the front door. She heard the politely muttered words exchanged between him and her grandparents and exited her room with a smile.

"Wow," Keegan said, standing with a smile of welcome as she entered the room. "You look awesome, Lacy."

"Thanks," she said. She waved a cheerful goodbye to her grandparents as she followed Keegan to his car. "Where are you taking me?"

"Wait and see," Keegan said, his chipper smile firmly in place.

"What is it with the people in your family, Keegan? Is no one ever in a bad mood?"

Keegan laughed, glancing at her in his peripheral vision. "Sure we are. I suppose we're too entrenched in our sturdy English Underwood heritage. You know—keeping a stiff upper lip, and all that." He glanced at her again. "With red hair and green eyes you're pretty much Irish, huh?"

"I don't know," Lacy said. "I recently found out my mother's adopted. I don't know much about my biological grandmother's family. Maybe she was Irish; she had strawberry blond hair and green eyes, too."

Keegan smiled. "You're touchy about having red hair. That's too bad; you're a beautiful woman, Lacy."

Lacy blinked through the front windshield, taken aback by his matter of fact tone. "Uh, thanks," she said.

The drive was short, so there was no time for awkward silence before they arrived at their destination. "Here?" Lacy asked, staring up uncertainly at her new building. Had Keegan not noticed the dirt, grime, and rodent droppings everywhere? She had a hard time not wrinkling her nose in disgust.

"Trust me," Keegan said. "I'm going to help you make peace with your new living space."

"That sounds ominous," Lacy said. She watched as Keegan unloaded an actual picnic basket from the back of his car before she followed him into the building and up the stairs to the roof. "Um, Keegan, I might not have mentioned this before, but heights and I aren't exactly friends."

"Don't worry about it," Keegan threw over his shoulder, which apparently meant he wasn't going to worry about it. He held the door of the roof for her, smiling coaxingly when she hesitated. "C'mon, Lacy. You're with a professional roofer; I won't let you fall."

"All right," Lacy agreed, hesitantly edging away from the door.

Keegan spread a blanket on the roof—disconcertingly far from the doorway—and began setting out food containers.

"Did you make all this?" Lacy asked, hunger overcoming her natural reticence at being four stories off the ground.

"I did," Keegan replied, humming absently as he dug in the basket for utensils and plates.

Lacy sat back, watching. Keegan and Tosh were both happy, settled people, but she felt somehow more at peace with Keegan. Maybe it was because she didn't have the pending pressure of trying to make a decision about the future of their relationship. Keegan didn't want anything from her but friendship. Did he? Her anxiety grew as she watched him unload crystal flutes and real silver. What man went to so much trouble for a woman he wasn't interested in? But he wouldn't be interested in her if Tosh was interested in her, would he? With a sinking feeling, her thoughts turned to her sister, Riley, always wanting what Lacy had.

Her head tipped to the side, studying Keegan as he worked. He paused in his setup to return her inspection.

"What's that look for?" he asked. "Are you analyzing me, Lacy?"

"Maybe," Lacy replied.

"Tell me what you find out. You could save me some time." At last he sat, unfurling his napkin with a flourish.

"Is this something you do often?" Lacy asked, indicating the elaborate picnic.

"Definitely. Women love picnics. I know all the right moves, Lacy." Instead of sounding cocky, he sounded sad, and Lacy wondered why. He gave her a wan smile. "Dig in before it gets cold."

She did as instructed, eating in silence as her mind continued to wander.

"So, what do you think?" Keegan asked after an extended silence.

"About what?" Lacy asked, drawn reluctantly from her meandering thoughts.

"The view." Fork in hand, he waved toward the horizon. "Isn't it spectacular?"

For the first time, Lacy really looked over the edge of the roof.

Night was descending. She could see the town and beyond to the hillsides dotted with brightly lit houses. Cars snaked through, adding their own small dots of light to the landscape.

"It's beautiful," Lacy remarked, taken aback not only by the view but by the fact that it was hers. She had never really owned much more than her computer and a camera before, and now she owned *this*.

Keegan set aside his empty plate and scooted close to her. "Imagine it on a warm summer night with some wicker furniture, some white lights, and the scent of flowers in the air. I know a guy who's a commercial landscaper. He specializes in living roofs. I'll give you his number."

As he talked, Lacy could picture it; she could see herself here on a summer night, relaxing on a piece of wicker, the scent of wisteria and lavender redolent in the air. The only dim spot in her fantasy was the blurry spot beside her. Who would share the spectacular view with her? Her grandparents?

"You don't look happy," Keegan noted.

"I guess it comes back to what I said before," she said. "This place is too much for me to handle by myself. I don't want to live here alone."

Keegan wrapped his arms around his legs, resting his chin on his knees. "There are worse things than being alone, aren't there?"

"Are there?" Lacy asked. "Worse than never finding that one right person? Worse than never having children?"

"I have to believe that there are," Keegan said, but he seemed to be talking more to himself than to her.

"Did you break up with someone recently?" Lacy asked. Maybe a bad breakup was the cause of his cryptic remarks and serious thoughts.

"I did," he said, sighing.

"Painful, huh?"

"Not really," he said. "We weren't serious; we were mostly just friends."

"Oh," Lacy said, confused.

"This is nice," Keegan said after a minute of silence. "Peaceful. Thanks."

Lacy chuckled. "You're the one responsible for this little piece of paradise," Lacy said.

Keegan leaned over, bumping her shoulder with his. "So you admit it's pretty much perfect up here."

"It could be," Lacy agreed, her thoughts wandering to her future again.

"Lacy, can I be uncharacteristically deep for a minute?"

Lacy smiled. He sounded so much like Tosh when he was about to tell her something "pastorly." "Go ahead," she urged.

"There's a lot of truth to the statement that you're not ready to be with anyone until you're ready to be alone. I sort of picked up on the fact that you're hurting. I don't think you're going to be able to move on until you heal what's happening inside of you."

"I don't disagree, Keegan," Lacy said, shifting toward him. "But how do you heal when you're hurting so much?"

Keegan rested his arm on her shoulder. "The age old question. But I think you're asking the wrong brother. Tosh is the one with all the answers."

Was it her imagination, or was his tone bitter? The sound of scrambling feet on gravel distracted her, causing them to turn and look behind them.

"Oh, geez," Jason said. He was in full uniform, one hand fisted on his hip, his flashlight held aloft. "I get a call about people on a roof, and I don't know why I'm surprised to find you here," he said, addressing Lacy. "From now on, any time I get a crazy call, I'm going to assume it's you." He shined the beam in Keegan's face. "Who's he?"

His abrupt tone wasn't Lacy's imagination, and it wasn't lost on Keegan who gave Jason the same infuriating smile that Tosh used whenever the two happened to meet. "I'm Keegan," he replied, clearly enjoying himself. "Who are you?"

"I'm the guy who's giving you exactly two minutes to get out of here," Jason said.

"Jason," Lacy tried to explain, but he interrupted by shining his flashlight in her face.

"Save the excuses, Lacy. I usually find teenagers up here making out. Imagine my delight to find you and him." The light bounced back to Keegan's face.

"But, Jason, you don't understand," Lacy said.

"And I don't want to," Jason added. "My fuse is this short tonight, Red." He held up two fingers pinched close together for emphasis. "Please don't make me do or say anything I regret. And may I remind you that this is the second time I've found you breaking and entering? Just grab your stuff and go." The light bounced back to inspect Keegan. "You from New York?"

"Chicago," Keegan replied, sounding totally unfazed as he loaded up his basket.

"Keegan is Tosh's brother," Lacy explained. She hoped her tone let Jason know their discussion wasn't over. He had plenty enough reason to be in a bad mood, but he didn't have to take it out on her and Keegan, especially when she owned the building in question.

"Figures," Jason said. "Just so I'm better prepared next time, exactly how many of you remain in Chicago?"

"Three brothers and two sisters, but some of those are married. And, really, not all of them are Lacy's type." Keegan finished packing and hefted the basket over his shoulder, giving Jason an impish smile. "This has been an informative meeting, Officer."

Jason didn't return his smile. Instead, he looked at Lacy and rolled his eyes. "Just get out and don't come back." He waved his flashlight, indicating that they should proceed in front of him.

Lacy swept by him without glancing at him. Tomorrow, when his terrible day was over and he was feeling better, she was really going to let him have it over his imperious attitude. She comforted herself by imagining the remorseful expression on his face when she informed him he had thrown her out of her own building. He held his flashlight for them, lighting the way as they walked down the rickety wooden stairs. Though she would never admit it, Lacy was glad for the light.

She wondered if Keegan had thought that far in advance or if, like Tosh, his intentions were sometimes better than his plans.

"Thank you for the escort, Officer," Keegan said, offering Jason a small salute. Jason didn't reply and his sober expression didn't change. Lacy paused in front of him and poked her finger in his chest, meeting the firm resistance of his vest.

"We are *so* not done talking about this," she hissed.

"Shocking," he said in the same dry, grumpy tone he had been using all night.

Lacy would have said more, but Keegan clamped a hand on her shoulder, tugging her toward his car. "C'mon, Lacy," he said. "No need to add assaulting an officer to your list of crimes tonight."

Still annoyed by Jason's blasé expression, she wanted to do something, anything to break through his annoyingly cool reserve, so she stuck her tongue out at him. Instead of making him angry, though, it made him laugh.

"Geez," he muttered, turning away as he closed and locked the door.

CHAPTER 9

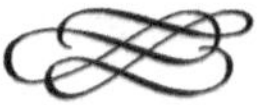

Morning came too early for Lacy. Though Keegan had gotten her home at a reasonable hour—even after repeatedly trying to worm information from her about her relationship with Jason—she still felt like she had just fallen asleep. At first she couldn't remember why it was important to wake so early, and then she remembered her meeting with Ed McNeil. She jumped out of bed, throwing her hair in a hasty ponytail. If she thought Ed McNeil was bad, he was nothing compared to his roadblock of a secretary. Lacy wanted to make sure and have the meeting over with before Pearl came back from the dentist.

For that reason, she bypassed breakfast. She would grab something later at the coffeehouse. Maybe the stop-work order would be resolved and she could make a few calls to some roofers to get the ball rolling on her building. Thinking of the calls she needed to make reminded her that she still hadn't heard from Tosh. She pulled out her phone and pushed the button, not surprised when it once again went to voicemail.

"Tosh, it's Lacy, that's L-A-C-Y. Why do I feel like I'm seeing more of your brother than I'm seeing of you? Whatever the reason, I don't like it, and I miss you. Please call me back." She gripped her phone, stuffing it back in her pocket with a sigh. Would there ever come a time in her life when there was total peace? When she wasn't in the midst of chaos?

Outside, the morning was brisk and Lacy picked up her pace to a trot—not enough to drench her in sweat, but enough to leave her breathless when she arrived in front of Ed McNeil's office. She bent over, gasping for air.

"Is that really how you run?"

Startled, she stood straight and encountered Jason. He was still wearing his uniform, though his face was unshaven and his eyes were bloodshot, not his usual clean-cut appearance by a long shot.

"Don't tell me you're still on duty," she said. Was he working a double?

"No, I got off a while ago." He turned, surveying Ed McNeil's office again.

"Jason, what are you doing here?" Lacy asked, laying a hand on his arm.

He jumped at her gentle touch, turning to look at her again.

Her heart wrenched as she once again glimpsed his bloodshot eyes. "Did you sleep yesterday before work?"

He shook his head. "There wasn't a lot of time after court, and I… just couldn't." He would have turned back to study Ed McNeil's office again, but Lacy caught his attention.

"Jason, don't do this. Don't confront him, or whatever it is you're thinking about doing. Go home and get some rest."

"That's probably a good idea," he said.

She frowned, disturbed by his vague tone and easy agreement. "You want me to drive you?"

That brought him out of his stupor enough to laugh. "No." His smile faded as they studied each other. Lacy moved her hand up to his bicep and gave it a squeeze.

"I'm worried about you."

"I'm fine," he said, and she wondered if he really believed it. He looked anything but fine; in fact, she had never seen him like this. Giving up on the pretense of keeping space between them, she edged closer and slipped her arms around his waist, bestowing a tight hug she hoped conveyed friendship and not desperation. He returned the hug, squeezing her tightly in return. For a few beats, they lingered that way, holding each other close, hearts beating in tandem. Maybe it was her imagination, but she thought she felt a bit of tension began to drain out of him.

"What are you doing tonight?" she asked, the sound muffled against his impressive chest.

"Is this a pickup?" he asked. His voice was muffled by the top of her head, where his face was now pressed.

"Depends on the answer," she said.

"I'm free," he said.

"Then, yes, it's a pickup. I owe you a meal. Maybe I could come over and cook something. Then we can talk."

"I don't want to talk," Jason said.

"Fine, we'll watch a movie."

Jason smiled again, easing his fingertips to her waist. "This is sounding better and better."

Lacy smiled, glad he was starting to sound halfway normal. "Are you working tonight?"

He shook his head. "It's my weekend."

"Is six okay?"

"Six is good," he said. He surprised her by capturing her hand and pressing it to his cheek, closing his eyes and taking a deep breath. "Thanks for this, Lacy."

"Maybe you should save your thanks until you taste my food," Lacy said, aiming for a light tone as she eased back and stared up at him.

When he opened his eyes, they looked more alive than they had a minute before. "It's not the food I'm thankful for. Later." He let her go and walked away, looking more exhausted than any person should.

"Be careful," Lacy called, glad it was only a few blocks to his house. He threw up a hand in recognition of her words, but otherwise didn't respond. After watching to make sure he got safely to his car without falling asleep, Lacy turned her attention back toward Ed McNeil's office.

"I'm going to get the stop-work order off my building," she said out loud, giving herself a little pep talk. "And then I'm going to let him know what he did to Jason was wrong." She pounded up the steps, gaining momentum along with her anger. "Then maybe I'll tell him his haircut is ugly. No one wears their hair slicked back like that anymore." She arrived at his doorstep and knocked briskly on the outer door, hurting her knuckles. Shaking her hand to get rid of the pain, she called through the door.

"Mr. McNeil, it's Lacy Steele. We had an appointment."

There was no answer. Undeterred, Lacy tried the handle and found it unlocked. "You can't ignore me," she said, though her words were bolder than her actions because her step was tentative as she poked her head around the door, searching for his secretary. Finding the room Pearl-free, she ventured farther inside. "Mr. McNeil," she tried again. "It's Lacy Steele." She knocked again, this time on his inner door. Maybe it was the eerie silence of the office, or maybe it was instinct, but she was suddenly nervous and ready to leave.

"Is this a bad time?" she said, gently pressing on the door so that it slowly squeaked open. He didn't reply, but she still had her answer; it was definitely a bad time. He sat in his chair, staring straight ahead, a small, neat hole in the middle of his forehead. Her eyes started to travel to the back of the chair, matted with gore, but she quickly turned away, not wanting to see. For a few beats, Lacy remained frozen, staring at his clock, not thinking or feeling anything at all.

Behind her, the outer door slammed, and Pearl's heavy steps clicked through the office. "What are you doing here?"

The question would have sounded harsher if not for the fact that her mouth was apparently still numb from the dentist, turning all her R's into W's. Still, her words had the desired effect on Lacy who snapped to attention and slammed the inner office door, not wanting Pearl to see the horror she had just witnessed.

"Call the police," Lacy said through lips that felt as numb as Pearl's must be.

"I will if Mr. McNeil tells me to." She marched to the inner door and prepared to open it. Lacy tried to block her way, but it was a futile attempt. Pearl was much taller, heavier, and larger boned. And she was angry. She grasped Lacy's wrist and yanked her out of the way.

"No, Pearl, please don't open that door," Lacy pled. This time she grabbed Pearl's wrist and tugged, bracing her feet against the floor to try and pull the larger woman back.

Pearl shook her off like a wet dog shaking off water droplets and opened the door. For a moment, Lacy felt sorry for her as a look of horror and immense sadness swept over her face. Then the pity was replaced by panic as Pearl turned to her, trembling with rage.

"What did you do?" she said. "What did you do to Eddie?"

"I...I didn't..." Lacy faltered, too shocked and muddled to think up a reply. However, when Pearl advanced on her, arms outstretched, Lacy's brain somehow snapped back to attention. *Run,* it told her, and she did. Not waiting to see what Pearl intended to do, she turned and began sprinting toward the door and freedom.

Pearl didn't keep her intentions a secret, though. "I'm going to kill you," she screamed, her voice as primal and terrifying as the sound of her heels clacking on the tile floor.

Fleetingly Lacy wondered over the fact that she was wearing sneakers and still somehow almost as slow as a woman wearing heels, but as soon as they reached the outer doors, something miraculous happened. Lacy's adrenaline kicked in, and it was as if she turned into FloJo as she sprinted down the steps in a graceful glide, her gait no longer hitched or slow. *This is why people run for pleasure,* she thought as she sailed along the sidewalk, her feet barely touching the pavement.

Behind her, Pearl was getting farther away, but that did nothing to temper her rage. She was still hurling insults and epithets. If Lacy weren't so thoroughly frightened, she might have laughed when Pearl yelled, "I'm going to snatch you bald, you little leprechaun," especially because the last two words came out "wittle wepwechaun." It was like being chased by a larger, female Elmer Fudd.

Ahead, Lacy caught sight of a black form, and she ran toward it as the beacon of hope it was. Tosh, standing on the sidewalk a hundred feet away in full clerical drag, stopped short and looked at her in alarm, and then he started jogging toward her. He reached her, grabbing her and holding her close when she buried her face in his chest.

"Lacy, what's wrong?" he asked, skimming his hands along her back and arms to check for broken limbs.

"She's trying to kill me," Lacy said, the sound muffled by his cassock.

"Who?" Tosh asked, and then looked up to see Pearl bearing down on them. "Whoa," he added, moving Lacy protectively behind him. Pearl barreled into him, so hard that he stumbled back, knocking Lacy to the ground. She sat there, stunned, as Pearl collapsed onto Tosh and began to weep.

Panting, wheezing, and seeing spots, Lacy pulled out her phone and called the police.

CHAPTER 10

Lacy's hand trembled when she knocked on the door. After she was finished, she clasped her hands behind her back and pasted on a smile.

Jason opened the door with a smile of his own, though he still looked tired and worn. He leaned against the doorframe, his arm stretched up so his hand curled over the top as his smile slowly faded.

"What's wrong with you?" he asked.

Lacy's eyes fluttered, trying in vain to clear away the sudden rush of tears. "Nothing." She eased by him, not waiting for an invitation to come inside, and went to the kitchen, depositing her grocery bags on his counter.

"No, really," Jason said, reaching out to lightly grasp her bicep. "What's wrong with you?"

His gentle touch was almost enough to break through her carefully contained emotions, so she shook him off. "Nothing. Did you sleep all day?" How else had he missed the news that there had been a murder?

"I woke an hour ago," he said, sounding wary now. "Are we arguing? Sometimes I lose track." He moved beside her and began helping unload groceries.

She shook her head. Clearing her throat, she tried to say it as casually as she could. "Ed McNeil was killed this morning. I found him." Her voice hitched as the mental image returned and she cleared her throat again.

Jason reached for the can of chicken broth she was holding, gently uncurling her fingers and setting it on the counter. He put his hands on her shoulders and turned her to face him. "What?" he said, stooping slightly to look in her eyes.

"I don't want to say it again," she whispered. Nervously, she licked her lips and blinked back more tears.

His thumbs smoothed over her shoulders, relaxing her so that she eased her stiff posture. "Then what happened?"

She omitted the part about Pearl chasing her down the street, and began instead with what happened when the police arrived. "Detective Brenner came," she said. It was the first time she had seen the man since she wrote her scathing article. She had expected open hostility and been surprised instead by his professionalism. "He didn't talk to me, just got to work taking statements and all that stuff you guys do. They," she paused and licked her lips. "They tested my hands for powder residue to rule me out as a suspect."

His hands tightened on her shoulders, but he didn't reply, knowing it had only been standard procedure.

"They didn't find any," she added, and that made him laugh.

"Of course they didn't," Jason said, giving her a little shake and a reassuring smile. She returned his smile and the silence stretched. "You had a very bad day," he said at last. Not waiting for her to reply, he slipped his arms around her and pulled her close, hugging her. Lacy responded by snaking her arms around his waist and nestling closer, enjoying the moment. They had never just hugged before; it was an intimate gesture devoid of the usual tension that always seemed to hum between them.

"I'm supposed to be cheering you up," she said, closing her eyes and breathing his scent.

"Believe me when I tell you this cheers me up," he said. Leaning down, he pressed a kiss to the top of her head. Lacy smiled. Inevitably, the tension returned. They seemed to feel it at the same time as their arms tightened on each other. There was always that moment of inde-cision; were they going to give in to it or fight it?

"Hungry?" Lacy asked, indicating a subject change.

"Okay," Jason said, his tone resigned as he let her go.

She moved away from him with a mixture of relief and disap-pointment. He sat at the table and watched while she worked, standing again to tie her apron after she shook it from her bag.

"You're the only woman I know who wears an apron," he said. He sat again, resting his chin in his hand.

Her first reaction was always to wonder what other women he was referring to, but she stopped herself from asking, not wanting to appear jealous. "I'm messy," she explained, her tone bordering on defensive.

"I didn't say I didn't like it," he added with whatever it was he infused in his tone that made her stomach clench. On her back, she could feel the heat of his gaze, but she didn't turn around. Unlike with Tosh, Lacy could never be completely at ease with Jason. They couldn't banter and not have it mean anything. She couldn't turn around and see a look in his eyes and not want to act on it. She had to be careful because she wasn't sure if she could trust him. Who was she kidding? She wasn't sure if she could trust herself.

Though they had never talked about the fine line that they walked, she knew Jason was as aware of it as she was. When he sighed, she wondered why. What did he want from her? What she told Tosh was true—she was still healing from her last relationship. But when she was with Jason, there was something more that held her back, some lingering insecurity from their past. Even though she was twenty six, there was still a little part of her that whispered, *Holy Cow! You're in Jason Cantor's house and cooking him supper. The Jason Cantor!*

"What's the smile for?" he asked.

"How can you tell I'm smiling when you can only see the back of my head?" she asked.

"Because I'm a cop and we're trained to notice these things. Also, I see your reflection in the toaster."

She shrugged, turning to give him what she hoped was an enigmatic smile. In reality, she would never admit she was smiling at the memory of every slumber party she had ever attended. Without exception, Jason's name had always come up at some point. They had gone to school together since kindergarten. He wasn't one of those kids who went through an awkward period and then became beautiful and popular. From elementary school on, he had been the "it" guy, the one all the girls giggled over and dreamed about. And now she, Lacy Steele—the girl who had rolled her eyes and hushed her friends from their silly daydreams, the chubby girl everyone had called "Annie" after an unfortunately short haircut—was standing in his kitchen cooking him supper. Could life get any more surreal?

"Let me help you," he said, standing to reach over her head when she strained for a high bowl. His chest brushed her back, warm and solid, and Lacy held her breath, fighting her ever-present panic, and finding it wasn't as hard as it used to be. Either she was adjusting to the idea of being near a man again, or she was adjusting to Jason. She wasn't sure which was more terrifying.

"Tell me something," she said.

"What?" he asked, resting his hip against the counter beside her as he crossed his arms over his chest.

"Something. Anything. Talk to me." *Talk me down off the ledge; reassure me that what we have going on here is just friendship.*

"What happened after you found the body? I got the feeling you edited something."

She looked up at him, her nose wrinkled at his perceptiveness, and he smiled smugly. "I ran for my life," she said.

He sat up straighter then, his arms dropping to his sides. "Why? Was the killer still there? You didn't mention...geez, Lacy," he smoothed a hand through his hair, tousling it. "It's like I can't leave you alone for a minute without you getting in some...ouch." He looked down, frowning, as she poked him in the side with a wooden spoon.

"No, the killer wasn't there. That would have been an important part of the story. His secretary came and chased me down the street."

He blinked at her, replaying the words in his head, and then he resumed his position with one hip against the counter again. "You know, a few weeks ago, I might have thought you were kidding. Now I know better. Why did she chase you down the street?"

"I don't know. At first I thought it was because she thought I did it, but on closer examination, I just think she's psycho." She told him the whole story of Pearl and her numb mouth, pausing a couple of times when he laughed.

"She actually called you a red-headed terror?" he said.

Lacy nodded. "Only it sounded more like, 'wed-headed tewwow.'" She poked him again. "Don't laugh. She did it in front of Detective Brenner and Tosh. It was very embarrassing. The woman hates me."

Jason's smile fled. "What was he doing there?"

"He's in charge of the investigation, I presume," Lacy hedged, returning to her salad prep.

"You know that's not who I mean," Jason said.

"He was just there," Lacy said, remembering her palpable relief when Tosh had caught and held her.

"He always is, isn't he?" Jason asked, his tone resentful. "And yet you made out with his brother."

"I did not," Lacy said, her temper flaring.

Jason smiled. "I knew if I asked you flat out you wouldn't tell me if you had. I'm going to try that technique on a suspect sometime." He reached around her, popping a piece of cheese. "So what is going on with you and the brother? You looked pretty cozy on that roof."

"We're friends," she said.

"Like you and I are friends?" he asked, quirking an eyebrow. "Like you and the pastor are friends?"

"We're all friends," she snapped, flustered by his insinuating tone.

"It would be interesting to know your definition of friendship as it applies to each of us," he said. "Care to fill me in?"

"Supper's ready," she announced.

"Of course it is." He reached above her again, this time for the plates. Instead of setting two places across from each other, he set them kitty-corner so they were sitting next to each other. Lacy glanced at the arrangement, remembering that Jason didn't like to eat alone. That thought led her to the image of him as a little boy. Had he eaten his meals alone then while his parents fought? He caught her looking at him and she smiled with all the sudden rush of warmth she was feeling. His smile was tentative in return, almost wary as he tried to figure out her sudden burst of emotion.

They filled their plates, carried them to the table, and sat. This time Lacy wasn't surprised when Jason rested his left hand on her knee, feeding himself with his right. How had she so quickly acclimated to his habit of touching her? She remembered her first meal here when he had told her that he was a touchy-feely person and she was going to have to get used to it. At the time, she had thought that an impossible feat. But now here she was, a few weeks later, and she didn't even feel awkward with his thumb trailing little circles around her kneecap. She felt many other things, but awkwardness wasn't one of them.

They ate in silence. Jason appeared lost in thought—though he did compliment her food—and Lacy was lost in sensation, enjoying his absent perusal of her leg. Maybe that was why she had so quickly warmed up to his touch, because it felt so doggone good.

"You're being unfair," he said after a few minutes of silence.

"Why am I unfair?"

"Because you want me to talk to you about what happened yesterday, but you've never told me why you're here, why you left New York."

He had a point, and she knew it, but that didn't mean she relished admitting her humiliating history. She tried to say it as matter-of-factly as possible. "I was engaged. He dumped me for Riley. We worked together and I found it impossible to stay, so I came here." Ran away, was a more apt description, but she figured he would read between the lines. He nodded and the silence stretched once again as they finished eating.

"It didn't start until after my brother died," Jason said at last. His voice was soft, and his eyes never left his plate.

Though she could barely hear him, she didn't ask him to speak up or repeat himself because she knew exactly what he was talking about.

"It's pretty common, I guess, for families to melt down after the death of a child," he continued. Resting his fork on the side of his plate, he sat back, dropping his hand from her knee. Lacy set down her fork, too, and pushed her plate aside, giving him her full attention.

"What happened after your brother died?"

"My parents started drinking. At first they did it together, getting drunk on the weekends after I went to sleep. They thought I didn't know, but I did. I guess they felt like it was okay because they were doing it together. Maybe they thought it was helping them heal, but it wasn't.

"After a few months, the drinking got worse and they began to turn on each other. The recriminations were awful, the blame they tried to lay on each other when it was no one's fault. It was a downward spiral that quickly got out of control. The yelling progressed to physical fighting. I know McNeil made it sound like there was constant abuse, but it wasn't like that. It wasn't one of those situations where my dad was beating on me and my mom; they beat on each other. It was mutual."

As if that makes it any better, Lacy thought. "And where were you during all this?"

"I was here," he said, sounding old and weary. "Trying to make sure they didn't kill each other. When I was little, I would cry and beg for them to stop. As I got older, I tried to physically insert myself between them. When I couldn't, I called the police. They were the only ones who could help, the only ones who could restore order, the only ones my parents would listen to."

Lacy reached out and clasped his hand. He squeezed hers tightly in return, staring at their fused fingers. "What about the part where they hit you?"

"My mom never hit me. My dad did a few times, but never on purpose. He was just so out of his head wasted that he had no idea who I was. He would have decked Mother Theresa if she'd gotten in his way. He was always sorry; they both were. Eventually it was that sorrow that made them sober up. They both got help and dried out, but the damage was done. Neither of them were what you'd call topnotch employees during that time, and they were starting to get reputations on the local bar scene. They decided to move away and make a new start of things. They're doing pretty well now."

"But you don't see them," Lacy said. She moved closer and added her other hand to the mix, devouring his hand with both of hers in an attempt to offer solace.

"It's…hard," he said. "The memories from that time are still fresh. A lot was said and done, and a lot wasn't said and done. I basically parented myself. It was chaotic. The house was a sty. I never invited people over." He gave a mirthless chuckle. "People thought it was because my parents were so strict I wasn't allowed to have parties. What a joke. I could have done drugs in front of them and they wouldn't have noticed."

Lacy let go his hands and cupped his cheeks, standing as she arched forward and aimed for his lips before he stopped her.

"Don't kiss me because you feel sorry for me," he said, his voice hoarse.

"What if I just want to?" she whispered.

"That's acceptable," he said. His hands settled on her waist, reeling her in as she advanced. For once she had the height advantage. She enjoyed the way his face tipped up to meet hers. She brushed her lips softly against his and began applying the slightest pressure when someone pounded on the door.

Jason and Lacy froze. He squeezed his eyes shut, his hands curling around her waist.

"If that's a Girl Scout, I'm not buying any cookies," he declared.

"If that's a Girl Scout, you should check her for steroids," Lacy said. The knock sounded forceful, urgent.

"Just hold that thought, okay?" Jason asked, opening his eyes. "Don't retreat."

Lacy nodded, but already she was having second thoughts. What was she doing kissing this man in his kitchen? Or any man, for that matter, when she was so unprepared for the consequences. As if sensing her emotional backpedal, he clasped her hand, tugging her behind him to the door as if tethering her to him might help. He opened the door and they stared blankly at Detective Brenner and a couple of officers Lacy didn't know.

"Sorry to do this in front of your girlfriend, Cantor," Detective Brenner said unconvincingly as his scorn-filled eyes flicked to Lacy. "But you're under arrest for the murder of Ed McNeil."

CHAPTER 11

It was like a bad nightmare as Lacy stood there, Jason's shock matching her own.

"You can't be serious," Jason said.

"I am," Detective Brenner said and, to his credit, he sounded apologetic. Lacy wasn't buying it, though.

"Are you crazy?" she said, rousing from her stupor. "You can't believe Jason did this. What evidence do you have?" She remembered how when her grandmother was arrested, the case had been so full of holes it was laughable. Surely this was the same scenario.

"We have one witness who heard him threatening to shoot Ed McNeil and another who saw him outside his office this morning. That and preliminary ballistics show the bullet came from one of our weapons," Detective Brenner said, though he was looking at Jason when he spoke as if explaining himself to his colleague.

"Why are you taking him in? Why not question him and let him go until the ballistics prove he didn't do it?" Lacy said.

"Because there was this article in the paper, written by a certain nosy and bitter reporter, and now our department is under careful scrutiny," the detective replied. "We can't make it look like we're giving one of our own special treatment."

"But Jason didn't do it," Lacy said. "I saw him outside the office this morning."

"Great, now we have two witnesses," Detective Brenner said sourly.

"My point is that there was no blood on him. He looked normal." The officers, including Jason, looked at her sharply when she hesitated on the word "normal." He hadn't looked normal; he had been in a daze. But he had been exhausted.

The detective ignored her, turning his attention once again to Jason. "Where's your weapon, son?"

"It's locked in my desk drawer," Jason said. He sounded resigned, and Lacy was afraid.

"Jason, tell them you didn't do this," she said.

But he didn't. He remained silent and stoic, not looking at her as they waited for one of the officers to receive his gun. "It's been recently fired," the officer said, holding it out to the detective for his inspection. Detective Brenner looked to Jason for an explanation.

"I dispatched an injured raccoon this morning before my shift ended," he said. "I called it in and wrote a report. I didn't clean my weapon because I was dead on my feet. I intended to do it later."

"There," Lacy said. "There's a reasonable explanation. And, besides, why wouldn't he clean his gun if he murdered someone?"

"Lacy," Jason said. "Stop."

She knew she wasn't helping the situation, but she couldn't seem to contain her anger, fear, and frustration, especially because this time seemed different than with her grandmother. This wasn't a witch hunt; there was compelling evidence on the table. How was she supposed to disprove any of this when it was over her head to begin with? What did she know about weapons or forensics? As if reading her thoughts, Jason preempted her.

"I don't want you getting involved in this," he said.

"Jason," she began, but he cut her off, stepping forward to press his palm to her cheek.

"No," he said. "It's too dangerous, especially with me not here to protect you. Just let it go; let the wheels of justice churn. They'll match my gun against the bullet and realize it's not the same one, and then this will all be over. Please promise me."

"If it turns out to be that easy, then I won't get involved," Lacy said.

"That's not what I meant. Stay out of it no matter what." The officers and detective were growing impatient. Jason glanced at them and put his hands behind his back before turning back to her.

She shook her head, choked up at the unbearable sight of him being handcuffed.

"Lacy," he said, sounding angry now. "Stay out of it."

"I'll come see you," she promised. "We'll talk more." He was handcuffed and there were three other people in the room, but she didn't care. She stood on her toes and pressed her lips fervently to his. His lips clung for just a second and then it was over and they were hauling him away.

He turned to look at her once more over his shoulder and mouthed the word, *"Don't."*

She turned away, not wanting to see him loaded into the back of the cruiser. His house felt not just empty, but eerily so, as if the house was already mourning the absence of its owner. Lacy was tempted to stay the night, to sleep in Jason's bed, just to ease the lonely, empty feeling, but that was crazy. How would she ever explain it to her grandmother that she stayed at Jason's house? Instead she took her time closing up and turning off lights, making sure everything was perfectly tidy, exactly as Jason liked it. As an afterthought, she grabbed his keys from the hook beside the door. If he stayed in jail for any length of time, she would have to check his house and retrieve his mail.

He can't stay in jail, she thought. Television had taught her what jail was like for cops. He could be seriously injured or even killed if some of the people he had arrested ganged up on him, to say nothing of the misery and humiliation. *I have to do something,* Lacy thought. *But what?*

As if in answer to her question, her phone rang.

Before she could say hello, the abrupt voice of the town's local newspaper editor cut across the line. "Lacy, it's Len. There was a murder today, and the rumor is that they've made an arrest. I need you to take this one; I need some hard-hitting journalism and not Marjory's over-the-top enthusiastic writing style. I swear that woman would report about her own demise with exclamation points and smiley faces. Are you free? Can you do it?"

Lacy bit her lip. Jason had told her to stay out of it, but if it was her job to investigate, then surely he would understand, wouldn't he? *No, he'll kill you,* a little voice warned. "I'll do it," Lacy said, ignoring the little voice and her own common sense. Just like with her grandmother, she was too close to this case to be objective, but working for the paper would give her the access she needed to get things figured out. She hoped.

"Good," Len said. "Like everything in this business, I need it yesterday."

"I'll send you something as soon as I get home," she promised.

He paused. "How will that be possible?"

"Because I was the one who found the body and I was here when they made an arrest in the case," Lacy explained.

There was another pause, longer this time. "You sure get around. Okay, I'll expect it soon." He hung up without a goodbye. Lacy let herself out of Jason's house, making a mental list of what she needed to do. First she needed to write an article for Len. Today that would be easy because she had discovered the body and been present for the arrest. But then what? There was no way Detective Brenner would share information with her. In fact, he would most likely roadblock her at every opportunity. What she needed was someone on the inside, someone who believed in Jason's innocence and would be willing to help her.

She pulled out her phone and hit a button. "Travis, it's Lacy. Did you know they just arrested Jason for Ed McNeil's murder?"

"What? No way. That's crazy. How could they possibly think Jason would kill anyone? He's like the best road unit we have."

Lacy smiled. At five years younger, Travis felt something like hero worship for Jason, which was good because she was going to need his help. "Can you keep an ear out and keep me informed of what's going on? I need to get this figured out so we can all return to sanity."

"I'll do my best, but you know how it is. I'm just a lowly jailer; I don't hear much."

"You're being modest. You always have the scoop."

"Yeah, I do." He chuckled. "I'll let you know if I hear anything."

"Thanks," Lacy said. "I guess I'll see you tomorrow. Want some coffee?"

"Is the sky blue?"

"I take it that's a yes," she said.

"No, that was a legitimate question. I've been working so much that I've forgotten what it's like on the outside. There aren't any windows in the jail. Coffee sounds awesome. See you tomorrow."

"See you," she said. *Take good care of Jason. Let him know he's not alone. Give him a hug for me.* She laughed at the last thought, as well as Jason's reaction to it if Travis tried to carry it out, but her laughter quickly faded away as she pictured Jason in jail. How very humiliating. At least she knew that he would be well treated as long as he remained local. And he wouldn't be in there for long if she could help it.

Lacy plodded to her grandmother's car, glad she had chosen to drive for once. The last few emotionally draining moments had exhausted her. She would go home, write the article for Len, and go to sleep. Maybe in the morning everything would look better with a fresh perspective. Maybe Travis would call to tell her the sheriff's office realized their mistake and Jason had been released.

She was so tired as she drove home that she almost didn't notice the headlights riding her bumper. When she did notice, she was nearly home. Was it coincidence that whoever it was remained right on her tail, obnoxiously flashing his brights so that she either had to divert her mirror to the ceiling or be blinded?

The car followed her all the way to her grandmother's house. Belatedly she realized home was the last place she should have gone, but where else was there? Their town was surrounded by cornfields. She certainly didn't want to go out there, and it wasn't like she could go to the police station for help now that Jason was out of the picture.

Instead she simply turned into her grandmother's driveway and watched as the car, a dark sedan, drove slowly by. When she was sure it was completely gone, she got out of the car and went inside. She wished now that she hadn't volunteered to write the article for Len. Like the rest of her body, her brain was exhausted. But she had told him she would write it, so she turned on her computer, dashed off the article, and mailed it before falling into a dead sleep.

The next morning, there were a few blissful moments when Lacy forgot everything. She woke and lay in bed, staring at her ceiling with a half smile, trying to get her sluggish brain to remember something important. Her phone rang, pulling her fully awake as she lunged for the nightstand. It was Tosh's ringtone, but of course she didn't expect Tosh to be on the other end of the phone, and he wasn't.

"Tosh is worried about you," were Keegan's greeting words.

Lacy almost asked why, and then it all came rushing back. Jason had been arrested for the murder of Ed McNeil. "If he's worried, then why didn't he call me himself?"

"Who can understand the mind of Tosh? All I know is that he told me to call and check on you, to tell you, and I quote, 'I don't like the guy, but he wouldn't kill anyone.' I can only assume the cop in question is the same one who chased us out of your building."

"Yes, that's him." Now that her memory had returned en force, she felt a little queasy over the thought of Jason still in jail. What was she going to do to get him out?

"No offense, Lacy, but he seemed really angry to me. Are you sure he didn't kill anyone?"

"I'm positive. He's one of the kindest and most caring people I know."

"We're talking about the guy who looked like he wanted to rip my head off, right? Muscular, grumpy, totally in love with you, that guy?"

"He's not...grumpy," Lacy finished lamely. What exactly had Tosh been telling Keegan about Jason to make him say such a thing?

Keegan chuckled. "Yeah, well Tosh is. I've never seen him this grumpy, and I'm beginning to understand why. You've got quite the little triangle going here."

Lacy didn't have time or energy for this today. "I should probably go; I have a lot to do."

"Like what?" Keegan asked.

"Like figure out a way to get Jason out of jail."

"I'll help," Keegan volunteered.

"That's really nice of you," she said, even though she didn't really want his help. "But I don't even know where to start; I don't know what I'm going to be getting into."

"Sounds perfect. I need a distraction."

Distraction from what? She wanted to ask, and at the same time she didn't have the energy to care. Keegan was temporary and he was fun. Maybe he was the distraction *she* needed to keep from thinking about the sorry state of her life with one friend not talking to her and another in jail. "Okay. Meet me here in half an hour."

"Too late, I'm on your porch." She heard him knock, and then heard her grandmother open the door as they exchanged indistinguishable words.

"Be out in a minute," Lacy called down the hall as she hopped out of bed and jumped in the shower.

By the time she emerged, her grandmother was feeding Keegan a full breakfast. He looked up at Lacy with a smile as she took a chair and filled a plate. Her grandmother bustled around the kitchen, refilling food, juice and coffee as needed. Keegan tried to tell her to sit down and not worry about him, but Lacy remained silent. Her grandmother was happiest when she was feeding someone. Lacy knew she was pleased about Keegan's presence, taking it as a good sign that Lacy was meeting Tosh's family. Her joy would probably dim if she realized Tosh was currently not speaking to her.

After breakfast, Keegan led the way to his rental car and held the door for her. Once he was inside, he leaned over the console and fastened Lacy with an intense gaze that caused her to freeze in sudden fear. Was he going to kiss her? Because that would be awkward.

"I found this on your door when I arrived," he said, shoving an envelope into her fingers. She looked down at it, slowly pulling herself out of the little fantasy where Keegan was inappropriately kissing her. While she had worked up a speech about how she wanted to only be friends with him, she still felt a little disappointed, and that was crazy.

Her name was printed in heavy block letters on the outside of the envelope. With shaking fingers she pulled out a folded piece of white paper. "Let the Stakely building go," she read out loud.

"What does that mean?" Keegan asked.

"I don't know," she said. Who would care what she did with the Stakely building? Ed McNeil had put a stop-work order on it, but that was because of money, wasn't it? And, if it wasn't, then what had it been about? She was distracted by Keegan's hand on her thigh. She looked up at him in alarm, only to realize he was trying to tug something from beneath her.

"You're sitting on the paper," he explained. "I forgot to move it before you sat down. Sorry." He pulled the paper free and held it out to her. "Can you imagine my surprise when I learned that my brother, who has never in his life cared about reading the newspaper, is suddenly a daily subscriber? And then I actually look at the paper and see that you wrote the main article today. And so I say that if you're causing Tosh to actually take an interest in current events, then you're a good influence on him. Good job, Lacy."

She gave him a vague smile as she looked down at the paper in her hands and saw her name staring back at her. Even though their paper had a circulation of less than ten thousand people, Lacy always felt a little thrill at seeing her name in print. She skimmed her article for a second, making sure what she had written so hastily during her exhaustion the night before actually sounded okay. It was while she was skimming that she happened to see the article below hers, and it jumped out at her because it was about Jason.

"The trial of Joe Anton has been put on hold due to the fact that Anton's council, Ed McNeil, was murdered yesterday and the arresting officer, Jason Cantor, was arrested for his murder," Lacy read. She paused, looking at Keegan. "Doesn't that seem odd to you that two people involved with that case have been taken out of the equation?"

Keegan shook his head. "In a town this small, I would find it odd if everything wasn't connected. In fact, I'm surprised you aren't all cousins."

She smiled, her eyes traveling back to the article to skim some more, and then she did a double take, grabbing Keegan's arm in surprise.

"What is it?" he asked, leaning over her to peruse the article. He smelled good, she noted absently.

"The murder, Joe Anton killing Susan Pendergast, it happened in the Stakely building. Don't you think that's weird? I mean, there's this renewed murder investigation and then I get a warning note about the building. How could it not be connected?"

"How could it be connected?" Keegan said. "What would one have to do with the other? The murder was more than twenty years ago. It's not like there's going to be evidence in the building, and this Joe Anton guy was already convicted. He's the only one who could profit by having his conviction overturned. Is it possible that he somehow sent you the threat?"

Lacy shook her head, remembering the sad sight of Joe Anton from the day she'd observed the trial. "He's in jail, and he's frail."

"Frailty can be an illusion. His body might be frail, but his will strong. Look at Charles Manson—the man probably weighs a hundred pounds wringing wet, yet look at the power he wielded. Maybe someone is working for Joe Anton."

"I guess that's possible, but it doesn't make sense."

"I thought today was about getting some answers, so let's go get some answers." He faced forward and put his hand on the ignition before pausing to turn to her again. "How do we get answers? Where do we start?"

"I have no idea," Lacy answered honestly. "I know I need to talk to Jason, but visiting hours aren't for a couple of hours."

"Maybe we could talk to someone who can give us more information about the Stakely building," Keegan suggested.

Lacy brightened. "That's an excellent idea." She took out her phone and used it to look up an address. "We'll talk to Sheila

Whitaker. I don't know if she'll be home right now, but it's worth a try."

They drove to Sheila's house in silence. Lacy didn't notice the silence until they arrived because she was busy thinking, her mind running rampant in a hundred different directions as she tried to assemble basic facts and make sense of the senseless. But then they pulled in Sheila's driveway, and she realized Keegan hadn't said a word in twenty minutes. She put her arm on his to stop him from leaving the car.

"Keegan, you don't have to do this. You don't have to be a part of this. You can drop me here, and I'll walk to the jail. It's not far, and I walk a lot."

Keegan grinned, an irrepressible smile she was beginning to recognize. "Are you kidding me? This is the most fun and excitement I've had in ages. It's the distraction I've been searching for."

That wasn't the first time she'd heard him mention needing a distraction. She wanted to ask him why he needed a distraction, but she didn't. Now wasn't the time or place, and she didn't know him enough to push him over something he wasn't willing to talk about. Later, she promised herself, she would try to talk to him about what was bothering him because something clearly was.

"Ready?" Keegan asked.

"Ready," Lacy said. Together they stood on the porch and rang Sheila Whitaker's bell.

CHAPTER 12

After ringing the bell three times, Lacy almost gave up hope, figuring Sheila must not be home. Then the door was roughly jerked open and Sheila's tall form filled the entryway and, by her red-rimmed eyes, it was obvious she had been crying.

"Hi," Sheila said. Her voice was tremulous. She pressed a tissue-stuffed fist to her mouth and sniffed.

"Are you okay?"

Sheila nodded. "A very dear friend died," she said.

"I'm sorry," Lacy said. "Now's obviously not a good time to talk. We'll come back."

"No, wait," Sheila said. Her hand shot out and grabbed Lacy's arm in a death grip. "I would like to talk to you because you knew him, knew what a great man he was."

Lacy had a sinking feeling, but she had to say the words anyway. "Who?"

"Ed McNeil," Sheila said the name on a sob. She let go of Lacy's arm to cover her eyes.

Lacy looked at Keegan, but of course he had no idea how shocking Sheila's statement was because he hadn't known Ed McNeil. But to hear the unsavory lawyer described as a good man was surprising to say the least. Despite her copious weeping, Sheila stood aside to grant access to her house. Lacy and Keegan awkwardly shuffled past her, stopping short when they reached the living room.

"Please sit down," Sheila said, attempting to pull herself together.

Lacy and Keegan sat together on the couch while Sheila sat in a chair across from them and wiped her eyes once more. "I'm sorry, I'm just—it was such a shock. I appreciated your article this morning, Lacy. It was well written. I was sort of hoping you might consider writing a tribute to Ed for the paper, something that would tell what a wonderful man he was."

"Uh," Lacy said, shooting Keegan a desperate look. Keegan gave her a helpless look in return and she realized she was on her own. "I'm, um, not sure I'm the best person for that. I tend to stick to fact-based stories when I write."

"But it would be fact," Sheila said, her tone suddenly vehement. "Ed was one of the best...Did you know he was one of the biggest donors for the Society of American Downtowns?"

Lacy hadn't known that, and it didn't make any sense. "But, Sheila, he put a stop-work order on the Stakely building to try and stop me from fixing it." Lacy tried to say it gently so as not to disillusion Sheila about the man, but she needn't have bothered.

"I'm sure it was because he was making sure your motives were pure where the Stakely building was concerned," Sheila said. "He was a staunch supporter of our cause, and he had been managing the property for the city. He was such a good man."

"You had been friends for a long time?" Keegan asked. His tone was gentle and laced with none of Lacy's incredulity. He sounded like Tosh when he was in full pastor mode.

Sheila nodded, her eyes tearing up again. "He helped me through a very difficult time in my life. We were, um, very close for a while."

Lacy didn't need to use a lot of imagination to understand Sheila's hidden meaning. Obviously Sheila and Ed had been more than friends at one point. Lacy had to hide her grimace of disgust. *Really, Sheila? Because you could have done better.* It was probably best to keep those thoughts to herself and not add to Sheila's misery, but the thought of anyone finding Ed McNeil attractive was unbelievable.

Absently, she thought of Pearl and her devotion to Ed McNeil. What was it about the man that made the two women so blind to his faults? Lacy thought maybe it wasn't coincidence that Pearl and Sheila shared more than a passing resemblance. Was Ed McNeil's wife a large, masculine woman? If so, he definitely had a type.

Sheila cleared her throat and tried to get her emotions under control. "I'm sorry. I thought I was all cried out, and then I saw the article this morning and I just..." She paused, clearing her throat again. "What did you want to speak to me about, dear?"

"It's really not important," Lacy said. "It can wait. Clearly this isn't a good time for you."

"To be honest, I would enjoy the distraction," Sheila said.

Distraction was the word of the day, apparently, so Lacy plunged in. "I couldn't help but notice that you're something of an expert on the Stakely building. I was wondering if you could tell me a little more of its history, specifically around the time that it closed."

"It closed because of a murder," Sheila said. She leaned forward, clenching her hands in her lap. "Did you know that?"

Lacy nodded. "I learned that this morning when I read it in the paper. You can imagine that it's shocking to find out there was once a murder in a building I now own." Although, technically she now owned two buildings where someone had been murdered if one were to count Barbara Blake's house. Lacy pushed that unnerving thought aside for further inspection later.

"I can't believe all this is being rehashed again," Sheila said. She pinched the bridge of her nose, squinting. "Not now, when everything else is so..." She paused again, sucking oxygen the way Lacy's yoga instructor had showed her to try and calm herself. In Sheila's case it seemed to work because she sat back, slightly more subdued. "I'm not sure what more I can tell you than has already been reported. For so many years the case remained unsolved, and then Joe Anton was arrested and it was over. And now it's open again."

There was something in her tone, something that made Lacy think she was well-acquainted with the case. "Do you think Joe Anton is guilty of the murder?"

"I did believe that, but Ed was so certain he was innocent. Ed has always believed in his innocence, from the very beginning. He was devastated when he lost the case the first time. He was positive he was going to be able to overturn the conviction this time. Now I don't know what to believe. I can't believe this is happening. All the old wounds are opening again, and now Ed is gone."

"Sheila, I'm sorry to be so blunt, but I think I'm missing something. You seem to be somehow connected to the original murder case. Was Susan Pendergast a friend of yours?"

"No, Susan was my sister," Sheila said.

Lacy had to let that information assimilate a few beats, so she was glad when Keegan asked the question she was thinking. "Didn't it bother you that Ed McNeil defended the man who supposedly killed your sister?"

"Ed believed strongly that everyone was innocent until proven guilty," Sheila said. "He truly believed Joe Anton was innocent, and he wanted to find Susan's true killer."

Lacy couldn't wrap her mind around the two versions of Ed McNeil, the one she had met who seemed to care about nothing more than the almighty dollar, and the one Sheila Whitaker described, the one who was a defender of the weak and downtrodden. Whichever was the true man didn't matter right now because Lacy's sorrow for Sheila was genuine. Not only had she lost a friend, but now her sister's case was being reopened. That seemed a little too coincidental to Lacy.

"Do you think the two cases are connected?" she blurted.

Sheila's mouth hardened into a thin, angry line. "Yes, they're definitely connected. The person who arrested Joe Anton is the same person who killed Ed McNeil."

So much for believing in innocent until proven guilty. "Sheila, Jason Cantor is a good friend of mine and an excellent officer. There is no way he killed Ed McNeil, and there is no way he manipulated evidence to arrest Joe Anton. He's one of the best and most honest men I've ever met."

Sheila looked dubious. "With the kind of family life he had growing up? How could any good come out of that?"

Those were fighting words. Lacy could feel the cap on her temper flip open, but before she could blast Sheila with whatever was about to come out of her mouth without first being run through her brain, Keegan grabbed her arm and pulled her to a standing position.

"Thank you so much for your time, Miss Whitaker. I'm sorry things are painful for you right now. You've been helpful and informative." He shook her hand with the one that wasn't holding on to Lacy, and then he turned and marched Lacy toward the door, not letting her go until they reached his car.

Once they were safely in his car, Keegan turned to her and spoke. "She's grieving, and not just the loss of her friend, but also the renewed loss of her sister. Of course she's going to say stupid things. It's probably easier for her to blame your officer than to find any other outlet for her emotions."

Lacy took a breath and allowed her anger to drain away as she exhaled. "Tosh does that, diffuses my anger that way. Must be a family trait."

"It's a gift," Keegan said, grinning as he started the car. "Where to, Miss Marple?"

"I'm sorry, did you really just make an Agatha Christie reference? When did you turn into an eighty-year-old woman?"

"What can I say? I enjoy the classics." There was a pause in conversation while he drove through their town's only coffee shop, ordering a coffee for Lacy to take to Travis.

Lacy resumed making fun of him once they were back on the road. "Do you have lace antimacassars covering your overstuffed armchairs? Do you knit one, purl two?"

"And if I did, would you hold it against me?" He turned to smile at her in a heart-stopping way. He really was handsome. So handsome, in fact, that Lacy had to go over her mental list of why she wasn't interested in him as more than a friend. Her plate was too full right now, she was still in mourning over her former relationship and, most important of all, he was Tosh's brother. She would never, ever do that to Tosh. But even though she wasn't interested in Keegan, she could still appreciate how easy he was on the eyes.

"Then it would simply be a blip in your otherwise perfection. Seriously, Keegan, how is it that you don't have a girlfriend?"

His smile dimmed as he faced forward again. "I've been busy. How is it that you don't have a boyfriend? Oh, wait, that's right. You've got too many to choose from."

"They're..."

"If you try and insist they're friends one more time, I will swerve this car into a tree. Wake up and smell the testosterone; you're way more than friends with both of them. Let me tell you that, from an outsider's point of view, it's as painful to watch you try and vacillate between them as it is to see them pining for you."

"No one is pining," she insisted. "They both know where I stand, and I'm not vacillating. I'm not ready for a relationship. Why are we talking about me? I thought we were talking about you."

"Did you?" he smiled at her again and she knew the conversation was over, not least of which because they had arrived at the jail.

"You don't have to wait here," Lacy said. "I can call my grandfather for a ride." In truth, she didn't want him to go in with her, knowing that it wouldn't go over well with Jason. He would keep up his guard and refrain from telling her anything.

"I'll wait," Keegan said. "Out here," he added as if he could read her mind. "I brought a book." He reached to the back seat and pulled out a backpack, stuffed to overflowing with books.

"Agatha Christie?" she guessed.

He held up the title for her to read. "*Orthodoxy,* by G.K. Chesterton. Wow, that's some light reading. Enjoy." She escaped the car, his chuckle echoing behind her as she closed the door and walked to the jail.

CHAPTER 13

"How long have you been here?" Lacy asked Travis as she handed over his coffee.

"What day is it?" he asked, and she wasn't sure he was kidding. "Two more hours, and I'm free. Free to go home and sleep, that is. You know what other twenty-one-year olds are doing right now, Lacy? Not delousing people, that's for sure."

Lacy winced, not just for Travis who was obviously exhausted, but for Jason, too. "Jason didn't have to be deloused, did he?"

Travis wouldn't quite meet her gaze. "It's procedure. It wasn't any fun for us, either, though."

"I know," Lacy said. "I'm sorry, sorry about all of it."

He shook his head. "I've never wanted anything more than to walk into my sergeant's office and hand in my resignation when they brought Jason in. This is such a load."

"You'll feel better after you get some sleep," Lacy said. "And this Jason thing isn't going to last. We both know he didn't do it. This is only temporary until the ballistics test clears his name."

Travis didn't reply as he buzzed her through. She walked to the now familiar visitation room where she sat waiting for Jason. There was a moment of trepidation as Lacy wondered if he might not come.

She couldn't help but remember when she had visited her grandmother for the first time, and her grandmother had refused to see her. Her connection to Jason was even more tenuous and emotionally charged.

After a few minutes of waiting, the heavy metal door buzzed open and Jason walked through. He looked grim as he sat and picked up the phone. Lacy picked up her phone, waiting to see what he would say. Would he tell her how bad he was obviously feeling about everything?

"You're using the fact that Len wants you to write about this as an excuse to investigate, aren't you?" were his first words, and Lacy realized Jason wasn't grim because of his ordeal but because he was irritated with her. Again. Or maybe still. She wasn't sure how to respond, but he didn't give her much of a chance. "So are you here in an official capacity to interview me? Let's go, Miss Steele, what do you want to know?"

"I think it's uncanny the amount of connections between this current case and the Joe Anton case," Lacy said, hoping to shock him out of his grumpiness.

"What?" he said, gripping the phone tighter. "You've got to be kidding me."

"I'm not. Ed McNeil was his attorney then. You were the arresting officer." She took another breath to tell him about the Stakely building, but couldn't bring herself to tell him about the ominous note she had received that morning, knowing he would worry himself to death. "There are a lot of connections," she finished lamely.

"There are two connections, and it's just coincidence, Lacy. The Joe Anton case was a slam dunk, so much so that I can't believe it took the detective division so long to figure it out. The signs were all there, and I went where they led. The case was airtight. Ed McNeil defended a lot of people, and I've arrested a lot of people. Cases are bound to overlap in a small town." He took a breath and consciously relaxed his grip on the phone. "I know it's hard for you to wait around and do nothing, but I'm asking you to back off and wait for the ballistics to clear me. The test is failsafe, and it will prove the bullet didn't come from my gun. We simply have to sit tight and wait for that to happen."

"If you didn't kill Ed McNeil, then who do you think did?" Lacy asked, her heated tone revealing her frustration. *Sit tight. Back off.* As if. Lacy knew if the situation were reversed, Jason would be turning over every rock to clear her name. How could he expect any less from her?

"I have no idea," Jason said. "But there were tons of people with motive, his client list for a beginning. He often defended the lowest of the low, people who didn't exactly stick to any sort of code of honor. I don't know for sure, but there have been rumors swirling about him for years. If the rumors were true, then Ed wasn't exactly the upstanding citizen he claimed to be."

"Who saw him as an upstanding citizen?" Lacy asked.

"Everyone he wanted to. He was a game player, a big campaign contributor, and involved in several civic activities. He fooled a lot of people into thinking he was a great guy."

"Sheila Whitaker certainly seemed to think so."

Jason frowned. "How do you know Sheila Whitaker?" His eyes narrowed and he leaned forward. "Did you talk to her? Did you go to see her?"

"I did," Lacy admitted. "But..." before she could tell him about the Stakely building, he interrupted.

"Lacy, what do I have to do to get you to stay out of this?"

"Get out of jail," Lacy said. "Get out from under these charges. Until that happens, I'm not going to let it go, Jason." With effort, she ignored his glower and pressed forward. "I think Sheila was in love with him, but wasn't Ed McNeil married?"

"If the rumors were true, Ed was also a real ladies' man."

"Seriously? He was so...ew."

Jason chuckled. "I'm not going to disagree. I didn't get it, either. I assumed the rumors were untrue because, well, ew."

They shared a smile as they stared at each other, the thick glass partition between them. "You want to know something crazy?" Lacy asked.

"What?" Jason prompted.

"You make that jumpsuit look good." It was uncanny. *No one* looked good in cheap fluorescent cotton, and yet somehow Jason did.

He laughed and Lacy watched as some of the tension eased from his face. He shook his head, disbelieving. "I'm serious," Lacy continued. "I hope I never get arrested because can you imagine my hair with that orange? Talk about a sickening combination."

"Red, if you get arrested, believe me when I tell you that how you look will be the last of your worries."

"How bad has it been?" she asked.

He shrugged. "Awkward, but not awful. The guys are doing their best to make it bearable."

"I'm sorry this is happening, Jason," Lacy said.

"It is what it is," Jason said, which she interpreted to mean he was done talking about it. "I don't suppose I could ask you one more time to let this go and leave it alone."

"You could ask," Lacy said.

"At least promise me you'll be careful," Jason said.

"I promise," Lacy said.

"I don't believe you," Jason said, "because even though you try and avoid it, trouble has a way of finding you."

"Keegan is with me; he's helping me."

"And that's supposed to make me feel better? You and the pastor's beefy brother spending truckloads of time together?"

"Did you just call another man 'beefy'?"

He laughed and she watched a little more of the tension drain out of him. "You're an expert at changing the subject. The fact is that I'm worried about you."

"And I'm worried about you," she said. "I've watched television; I know what happens to cops in jail."

He laughed again. "Lacy, geez, what goes on in that head of yours? I'm in the safest place in the world, guarded by all of my coworkers, while you're out there with a murderer, one you are actively trying to pursue, and you're worried about *me*. Is it any wonder you make me crazy? I stay up nights just wondering what you're going to get into next."

"You stay up nights because you work the midnight shift."

"Not anymore," he said, the grim lines returning to his mouth.

"You will. This is all going to get cleared up and be a bad memory soon," Lacy said.

"If you tell me someday we'll laugh about this, I'm not sure I'll believe you."

"I wouldn't go that far, but we'll look back on it with a sense of relief that it's over and that it didn't last too long. I promise."

"I don't think you've ever made me a promise before," Jason said. He pressed his index finger to the glass.

Lacy reached up and pressed her finger on the other side. "Now the pressure is on to make sure I keep it."

"Lacy," he began, disapproval lacing his tone, but she didn't allow him to admonish her again.

"I should go. I'll come back tomorrow, unless this is all over and you're not here."

"I'll see you here tomorrow," Jason said. Lacy hated the resigned tone in his voice. As he finished speaking, another woman shuffled behind Lacy, her tiny tank top stretched tight over her ample bosom while her skirt barely reached her thigh. Jason and Lacy paused to watch while she wiggled to the empty space beside them, tottering precariously on her too-high heels.

"Would it make you feel better if I wore something like that when I come back tomorrow?" Lacy asked, turning to face Jason once the woman was finally seated.

Jason laughed and shook his head. "Do you actually own anything like that?"

"No, but I could ask her if I could borrow something. I don't know her, but I'm pretty sure we're bonded now by this mutual experience. Soul sisters, if you will."

Jason glanced at the woman again. "I arrested your soul sister last week for drunk and disorderly. I think I would prefer that you stay away from her, tempting as your offer is."

He was smiling, and that was her goal. She wouldn't have been able to leave him if he had looked sad or upset. "I guess I'll stick to my usual sweater and jeans," Lacy said.

"I happen to like you in a sweater and jeans, but then I haven't seen you in anything I don't like."

"I'm going to leave on that high note," Lacy said.

"See you, Red."

"See you, Jason." She stood and walked away, leaving him smiling in her wake.

Lacy had spent so long visiting Jason that she wondered if Keegan would be irritated. When she reached the car, however, he closed his book with a smile. "Hungry? I'm starving. Do you care if we grab some lunch?"

"Lunch sounds great."

"Where do you recommend?" he asked.

She mentally reviewed the town's lackluster lunch offerings. "The taco place, I guess."

"This town has a taco place?" he asked.

"Don't get too excited—the owners are Italian, so I'm not sure how authentic it is. The food's pretty good, though."

They made the short drive to the taco place in silence. Lacy was hungrier than she realized, feeling almost faint from not eating. "I'm sorry that took so long," she apologized. "You must be starved."

"Don't worry about it," Keegan said amicably as they stood in line. "How did it go? Did you find out any new information?"

"No. Jason doesn't want me to be involved in this. He's not likely to be cooperative."

"No offense, Lacy, but this isn't exactly Chicago. What's the worst he thinks could happen to you?"

"I could get killed. A lot goes on here. You'd be surprised by how much crime there is. Jason's not just window dressing, he serves a purpose."

Keegan was looking at her with a combination of alarm and amusement and she realized how defensive she sounded. "Sorry," she added. "I think I'm hangry."

"Hangry?"

"Anger caused by hunger," she defined. "Hangry."

He smiled. "You are definitely just what the doctor ordered for me this week. Good thing Tosh is leaving me to fend for myself so much so I can spend all this time with you."

He turned to stare at the menu board while Lacy studied him. What was he talking about with all those cryptic little remarks? Before she could ask him, someone called her name.

"Yoo-hoo, Lacy."

Lacy turned to look at the interior of the crowded restaurant and saw Rose and Gladys, two of her grandmother's friends. Gladys had her hand in the air, waving Lacy over. "Come join us," she called.

Lacy nodded and forced a smile. "Prepare yourself," she muttered to Keegan. It wasn't that she didn't like her grandmother's friends; it was just that she wasn't certain about them. Sometimes they seemed as sweet as her grandmother, and other times they reminded her of the quintessential mean girl clique they had once been in high school, pretending to be nice to her face while shredding her behind her back.

They received their food and Lacy led the way to Rose and Gladys. They were leaning forward, staring at Keegan so intently Lacy expected one of them to pull out a magnifying glass for closer inspection.

"Who's your new young man?" Gladys asked.

"This is Keegan Underwood," Lacy said. "Tosh's brother."

The fact that he was their pastor's brother did nothing to lessen their speculation. If anything, it increased it. Lacy felt a little bad for Keegan as the women pounced on him, questioning him about personal details of his life but, like Tosh, Keegan seemed to have a way with women. Soon he had somehow answered all their questions without revealing anything at all, and they were now smiling at him in approval.

Their beaming smiles dimmed as they turned to look at Lacy and back again. "Does Tosh know you two are together?" Gladys asked.

While Lacy searched her mind for a polite response, Keegan beat her to the punch. "Of course. Why do you think I'm here? One of us had to be dispatched to meet this Lacy he keeps talking about."

Lacy fought a groan. Did he have any idea how that sounded to these women who took more of an interest in her love life than she did? By his mischievous grin, she thought maybe he did.

"Now is a good time while her other one is in jail," Rose said. "Looks like he's going to be there for a long time, too."

"I don't think so," Lacy said. "He didn't do it, Rose. He's going to be out as soon as the ballistics test comes back."

"I hope so," Rose said sincerely. "He's always seemed like a good boy."

"Lacy seems to think that this case is related to another murder that happened over twenty years ago," Keegan said. "I bet you ladies know a lot about that one."

Lacy beamed at him for his brilliance. Not only would talking about the Susan Pendergast murder take the focus off of Lacy, but she might actually glean some information from Rose and Gladys. She sipped her soda while the two older ladies sat up, preening importantly.

"It was so long ago," Gladys began. "Who can remember every detail, although it was pretty awful. Susan was a nice girl, from a nice family. Not like her sister."

"What's wrong with Sheila?" Lacy asked.

"She was always the wild one," Rose said. "Boy crazy, headstrong, different."

Lacy tried to imagine Sheila as wild and boy crazy, but the image wouldn't form.

"I thought when she got married she would settle down," Gladys added. "But that didn't last very long." She leaned forward and dropped her voice to a whisper. "Her husband left her for another woman."

"Maybe the death of her sister left an indelible impression. Sometimes grief can make people do crazy things," Lacy said. She was thinking of Jason's parents and their total meltdown after their son's death.

Rose shook her head. "From what I heard, the two sisters never got along. There was bad blood between them from birth. In fact, at the time of the murder they weren't even speaking."

Lacy shifted in her seat, uncomfortable with how closely the description fit her and Riley. How would she react if something happened to Riley before they resolved the issues between them? "What were they fighting about?"

"A man," Gladys answered. "Isn't it always a man?"

Rose darted a furtive glance around the crowded restaurant before leaning closer and whispering as Gladys had done. Unfortunately Rose's hearing was going, so her whisper wasn't exactly quiet. "And not just any man. They were fighting over the mayor."

"Rose," Gladys exclaimed. She jabbed her friend in the arm and looked around to see if anyone was listening. "You shouldn't gossip about the mayor."

"He wasn't the mayor then," Rose said, rubbing her arm and frowning at Gladys. "His father was mayor," she continued, addressing Lacy and Keegan again.

"Was he looked at as a suspect at the time of the murder?" Lacy asked. She didn't bother to whisper because Rose wouldn't have been able to hear her.

Rose shrugged. "There were questions, but his daddy had the whole thing hushed up. Most people in town figured he did it, until that other man was arrested."

"But he's been our mayor since before Joe Anton was arrested," Lacy said, aghast. Had people really voted for someone they believed could be a murderer?

"His father was mayor," Gladys said as if that was reason enough for his son to be elected.

"I don't understand why the Stakely building was closed because of the murder," Lacy said.

"The building had started to deteriorate," Gladys explained. "The owner was old and unable to keep up with the repairs. Things were in sad shape—it was most likely going to close anyway. And then there was all the crime."

"Crime," Lacy repeated. "What crime?"

"Lots of thefts, break-ins, and robberies," Gladys reported. "The town had a lot more young people then, and we were having a real drug problem at the time. For some reason all the druggies liked to hang around in the parking lot of the Stakely building. There at the end they had to have extra security. The police were working a lot of overtime trying to keep the crime away. And then Susan was murdered. If you ask me, it was high time they closed it. I wish they'd tear it down. Too many bad memories."

"I bought the Stakely building," Lacy said. Rose and Gladys stared at her as if she had just announced she was moving to Mars to set up a colony.

"Well, I think that's great," Rose boomed at last. "I don't agree with Gladys. The Stakely building's good memories outweigh the bad. It was a nice place before it fell into disrepair. Plus, this will be a good project to take your mind off your sister stealing your fiancé."

The last part was said during one of those strange and collective lulls that sometimes happens in a public place so that seemingly everyone in the restaurant turned to stare at Lacy.

Gladys jabbed Rose again. "Rose, Lucinda said not to mention that because it makes Lacy sad, especially since Riley got engaged. We don't want Lacy to start eating and get chubby again."

Lacy happened a glance at Keegan, expecting to see pity, but instead she saw amusement. He was eating with forced concentration to try and hold back a laugh.

"That's true," Rose said, rubbing her arm where Gladys had poked. She was going to have quite a bruise in the morning. "She'll never get a man if she gets big again."

"Now that's just not true," Keegan said. "I think Lacy could get a man no matter what size she is." He finished his last bite and rested his arm on the back of Lacy's chair.

"Maybe so," Gladys said, tipping her head as she studied Lacy. "She does have a string of them, and she's not exactly what you'd call thin."

"She has a nice figure," Rose belted. "Lots of curves. Men like that. They only pretend to like those stick-thin women. When it comes right down to it, men want a woman with childbearing hips. Lacy has those."

From her peripheral vision, Lacy caught the man at the table beside her staring speculatively at her hips. She was always at a loss about how best to deal with her grandmother's friends. She didn't want to be disrespectful, but she had to make them stop talking about her as if she were a pig at market.

"I think men are looking for more than childbearing hips," she said at last, whispering in a vain attempt to get Rose to lower her voice.

No such luck, though. Rose and Gladys exchanged a look, one that seemed to agree about Lacy's naïveté. Finally it was Rose who spoke again. It seemed to Lacy that she was yelling now, but maybe mortification made everything seem louder.

"Face it, Lacy, when it comes right down to it, for men, it's all about sex."

CHAPTER 14

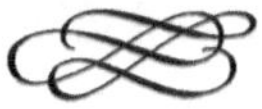

"If someone created a pill that could erase your memory, they could make a lot of money."

Keegan laughed as he maneuvered the car out of the restaurant's parking lot. "It wasn't that bad."

"You're just saying that because it wasn't about you. I don't know why my grandmother's friends are under the delusion that my life is their business, but somehow they feel the need to make commentary on it at every opportunity. I mean, my grandmother doesn't do that. She doesn't butt in, ask nosy questions, or offer unsolicited opinions. Why do her friends?" Lacy picked up the newspaper and fanned her flushed face. She couldn't remember the last time she had been so embarrassed.

"Maybe it's their misguided way of trying to show you they care. Or maybe they're just bored and lonely."

"Or the third option—they know exactly what they're doing and like to see me squirm."

Keegan shrugged. "Before witnessing that little scene I might have disagreed with you, but I've never seen such an old woman yell 'sex' so loudly before."

"Thanks for getting me out of here," Lacy said. While she had stared dumbly at Rose, trying to think up a reply, Keegan had said their goodbyes and gotten them outside.

"So that's the big mystery, huh? The reason you won't date my brother or the other guy. You were jilted for your sister."

"Don't try and put it delicately to spare my feelings," Lacy said.

"I wouldn't," Keegan replied. "I believe in dealing with things head on, at least when it comes to other people. Besides, if you keep tiptoeing around the facts and your resulting feelings, then you're never going to move on. Call a spade a spade—the miserable loser dumped you and broke your heart."

There was a little part of Lacy that did feel relieved to have things so blatantly laid on the table. "You know what the worst part is, though? It's that the situation is too complex for me to just get over. I feel like if he had dumped me for a stranger, I could grieve and then move on. But since he dumped me for my sister, the grief never goes away. I'm confronted with it every day. And then I have to add in her betrayal. Sometimes it seems like I'm never going to get over it."

"Do you want to?"

"Of course I want to," Lacy said.

"I know you want to in the rational sort of way that we're always supposed to want to get over things and move on. But don't you think there's a little part of you that's enjoying being the wounded party, that's enjoying wallowing in your misery? It's not often that you get to be the victim not only of a man, but of your rival sister."

"That's just a really horrible and sexist thing to say, like all women are dying to be the tragic romantic heroine of their own love stories."

"Aren't they?" Keegan asked.

"No! I didn't want this; I wanted to live happily ever after. Now I'm *here*." Her hand waved toward the window, indicating a cornfield to her right.

"Okay, I'll admit the town is small, but it's not as boring as I first thought. There's been a murder, and you're in the middle of it. You're the town's go-to journalist for hard-hitting news, and you own the biggest building in town. Maybe this isn't the life of your dreams, but it's still your life. You have the chance to do something great here, to be something amazing."

Lacy sat back, thinking. "There's a part of me that agrees with you. It's like I can almost see the person I could be, this exciting, strong, adventurous woman who is more resilient for having suffered a heartbreaking setback. But it's like looking through a glass darkly. I can't quite make it out, and I have no idea how to reach it, how to be that person. All I know right now is that I'm hurt and confused, but I don't want to be hurt and confused. I want to move on, but I don't know how."

"I think you're doing it, and you just don't know. I mean, you've already established relationships with Tosh and the officer; that's a start. Maybe you're not where they want to be, but you're where you should be. And you're not wallowing; I was being hyperbolic when I said that. You're working for the paper, and you bought a building that you're going to renovate. That's a huge project for anyone, let alone a twenty-six-year old. I guess my motivation for wanting you to move on is twofold: I want you and Tosh together, true, but I want you to be whole again for you. I really like you, Lacy." He smiled at her, one of those heart-melting smiles that had probably made count-less women swoon. "So what's next in your investigation, Inspector Steele?"

His question snapped her out of her trance, the one that had been induced by his hypnotic good looks. "I have no idea. Nothing makes sense. I can't tell if it's wishful thinking that makes me want these two cases to be connected. Maybe it's a whole lot of coincidence that Ed McNeil and Jason are connected to two cases, both of which are connected to the Stakely building when I start receiving threats about it."

"Speaking of threats, I think we're being followed." Keegan was looking in the rearview mirror as he spoke. Lacy turned around and saw a dark sedan.

"I think that's the same car that followed me last night."

"You have to report this," Keegan said.

"I can't. I'm not exactly on the sheriff's department's nice list right now. They're sort of upset over this article I wrote, and the head detective especially hates me."

"It's uncanny how someone so sweet has so many enemies," Keegan said. He swung a sharp right and glanced in the mirror. The car followed. "Hold on," he said. "I'm about to get fancy."

Lacy did hold on because Keegan sped up before slamming on the brakes and jerking the wheel to the left, swinging the car in a wide arc. Thankfully the road was wide and deserted, except for the other car that was now speeding toward them. They passed the car and Lacy craned her neck, trying to see inside, but all she saw was a tall figure behind a hat and sunglasses.

"Did you see anything?" Keegan asked.

"It's clearly a human." She sat back down and buckled her safety belt. "Where did you learn to drive like that?"

"*Grand Theft Auto.*" He glanced in the rearview mirror again. "I think that did it. They're not following anymore. And I got the plate. Write this down." He paused while she found a pen and scribbled the plate number on a piece of paper. "Obviously whoever it is knows where you live, so they're not following you to find out that information, which means they're following you to intimidate you."

"It's working. What am I supposed to do?"

"Why don't you stay with me and Tosh tonight?" Keegan suggested.

"I can't do that. You saw what lunch was like with Rose and Gladys. Can you imagine what the gossip mill would be like if I stayed over at Tosh's house?"

"You can't live your life worrying about what people say," Keegan said.

"I'm not worried for me—I'm worried for Tosh. It's not my professional reputation on the line, it's his. He's young, and I get the sense that people are waiting for him to fail so they can run him out of town with lanterns and pitchforks at the first hint of impropriety."

"Tosh can take care of himself," Keegan informed her. "It's you I'm worried about. Speaking of which, where are we going? We've been driving for a half an hour, and I still don't have a destination."

"Let's go to the library so I can look up the articles about the original murder. They haven't been converted from microfilm onto the web yet, so it's going to take a few minutes."

"No problem, I'm at a good point in my book."

He sat in the reading room of the library while Lacy found the article and made copies. When she was finished, she invited him to her house to go over everything. Her grandmother set out plates of cookies—which Lacy studiously avoided since she didn't feel like taking a run—and Lacy spread out the copied articles from the Pendergast murder.

"There's nothing more than what we already knew," Lacy said, frustrated enough to reach for a cookie before stopping with her hand in midair. "The author's article goes over everything in greater detail. The Stakely building had been having crime issues, and security was heightened. Susan Pendergast was working late at a shop that sold macramé artwork. Nothing was missing from the store or from Susan's purse, and there was no sign of a struggle. Although, here's something interesting: the person who wrote the original article was my editor, Len, and the responding officer was a young Detective Brenner. Of course he wasn't a detective then." She paused, frowning. "It's hard to picture either of them young." Looking down, she resumed skimming.

"On a personal note, the article does state that Susan and Sheila were sisters and that Susan was dating the mayor's son at the time, the man who is now our current mayor. There's a drawing of where the shooting took place in the Stakely building, but there's no mention of Ed McNeil, and certainly no mention of Jason who was only a toddler at the time. There's no obvious connection here, and yet my intuition tells me that there is a connection. I just can't see what it is."

"Why don't we write down everything we know about each of the cases and see what overlaps," Keegan suggested. Lacy noted with a sigh of relief that he finished off the last of the cookies. Temptation was abated, at least for the moment.

"Good idea," she said. He was turning out to be as good a sounding board as Tosh who often listened when she thought aloud, offering up helpful ideas and solutions. She took out a piece of paper and made two columns, one for the old murder and one for the new.

In the old column, she had Susan, Sheila, the mayor, Joe Anton, Ed McNeil, and the Stakely building. In the new column she had Sheila, the mayor, Ed McNeil, the Stakely building, and Jason.

"Do you think I should put Joe Anton in the new column, too, since it was his retrial that was interrupted?" Lacy asked.

"Honestly, I don't know what should go in the new column. All we know for certain is that Ed McNeil was killed, and Jason stands accused. Everyone else is extraneous."

"No, I have to include the Stakely building because it's somehow a part of all this, and if I include the Stakely building, then I have to include Sheila, who's the head of the SAD, and the mayor who was so vehemently opposed to selling it to me. There's too much coincidence for things to be a coincidence."

"Don't forget to add whoever is sending you the threats to our current list. If the Stakely building is involved, then so is whoever doesn't want it to be sold."

"That raises another interesting question: why did Ed McNeil put a stop-work order on the building if Sheila said he was such a proponent of its preservation?" Lacy asked.

"I have no idea. We're missing too much information. Know where we can get some more?"

"Maybe." She picked up her phone, found the number she wanted, and called the mayor's office to request an appointment. The mayor's secretary told her an appointment was impossible until Lacy informed her it was about the Stakely building.

"He'll see you first thing tomorrow morning," the secretary informed her when she came back on the line.

"You're going to be there, aren't you?" Lacy asked. "You don't have a dental appointment or anything?"

"No, I'll be here," the woman said. Her tone was wary now, as if she were dealing with a nutter, but Lacy wasn't taking any more chances of finding another dead body. One was more than enough for this lifetime.

After she hung up with the mayor's office, she called Travis. "How do I visit with Joe Anton?" she asked with no preamble.

"Show up and ask to see him," Travis said on a yawn.

"Do you think he'll see me?"

"I think he'll try, but he's so delusional he'll probably think he's having a conversation with the Easter bunny. The man is a walking commercial for saying no to drugs. Talk about a fried brain."

"It can't hurt to try," Lacy said. "I'm getting a little desperate. Do me a favor and don't mention my visit with him to Jason, okay?"

Travis chuckled. "Lacy, I don't mention you to Jason at all. I learned my lesson the hard way after the first time."

"What's that supposed to mean?"

"Let's just say Jason isn't crazy about hearing your name on another man's lips. Even after your article came out, the one about Detective Brenner, no one dared mention it to Jason. Everyone knew better."

Lacy let out a breath. "That stupid article. Was it pretty bad there? Does everyone hate me?"

"Yes and no. There's this code, you know, one that I am in clear violation of for talking to you about stuff that goes on here. But on the other hand ever since your article came out, Detective Brenner has been like a whole new person. He's Mr. Professional now. I think you scared the life back into him. Rumor has it that he was a good cop once upon a time."

"I hope something good came from the stupid thing, and I hope everyone will eventually forgive me for writing it. I don't believe one bad apple ruins the whole bunch. I have nothing but respect for the other deputies."

"It'll be fine," Travis said. "'Cause, see, there's this other code where none of us is allowed to hate a fellow officer's woman and you, Lacy, are most definitely Jason Cantor's woman."

"Well, that was…archaic."

Travis laughed. "I guess I'll see you tomorrow."

"You'll see me," Lacy promised. "I'm about to become a thorn in someone's side until this mess gets cleared up; I just haven't figured out whose problem I'm going to be yet."

"I'm not sure if I pity the person or envy him," Travis said.

"Pity, Travis, definitely pity."

CHAPTER 15

Lacy was groggy the next morning. Keegan had stayed for supper the previous night and left reluctantly at Lacy's urging. It suddenly occurred to her that he hadn't spent any time with Tosh, and maybe that was why Tosh was upset with her. After Keegan left, she stayed awake long into the night, reading and rereading the articles from the Pendergast murder and going over her charts, looking for some further connection between the two cases. There was a missing link, but she had no idea what it was.

Keegan had volunteered to come early and take her to the mayor's office, but Lacy decided to drive herself, hoping that by doing so Keegan and Tosh would get some more time together.

When she went into the kitchen, she heard a strange noise coming from the front porch. Opening the door, she saw her grandfather with his hand in a bucket of soapy water.

"It's a little late in the season to be cleaning windows," she said. Not to mention how early in the day it was.

Her grandfather sighed and dropped the rag in the bucket. Straightening, he beckoned her outside. "I was trying to clean this before you woke up and saw it."

Lacy stepped out onto the porch and turned to face the front door. There, spray painted in large red letters, were the words "LEAVE THE STAKELY BUILDING ALONE." Lacy sighed. "I'm so sorry about this."

"It's not your fault, Lacy," her grandfather said.

"You don't have to fix this. I'll do it." She reached for the bucket, but he intercepted her with a hand on her arm.

"I want to do it. Go back inside and eat your breakfast. I became really adept at removing graffiti when I was a principal. This is like a walk down memory lane." His cheerful tone and smile did little to hide his worry, and Lacy felt bad all over again, especially when she walked inside and saw that her grandmother had made cinnamon rolls—her standard I'm-too-worried-for-words-so-I'll-stuff-you-with-cinnamon-and-sugar food.

"Good morning," Lucinda said. Her tone was overly bright and cheerful, too, as if the two grandparents had agreed not to mention a word about anything unpleasant. Lacy went along with them, eating her cinnamon roll—or two—in silence.

When her grandfather came inside, though, she decided it was time for a talk. She waited until he retrieved his coffee and sat before starting. "I think it would be best if I moved out," she said.

Her grandfather put down his coffee, and her grandmother sank into a chair. "Because of the paint?" Lucinda said.

"Partially. I can't ignore the fact that I've put you in danger, and that's unacceptable. But, besides that, don't you want some time alone? You're in a relationship now. It's got to be uncomfortable to always have me around."

Her grandmother turned to her grandfather, deferring to him because she seemed at a loss for words. Mr. Middleton blew on his coffee and took a sip before answering. "Lacy, you're viewing our relationship with the rosy glasses of youth. But Lucy and I aren't kids anymore, and we're not in that stage where we want to spend copious amounts of time alone together. We're in that stage where we realize that nothing is more important than our family, and that's you. We love spending time with you. If you want to move out, then do it because it's what's best for you. But this is your home, and there's no need to move on our account."

Her grandmother was nodding furiously by the end of his speech, and Lacy smiled. "But I've put Grandma in danger. That's unacceptable."

"Lacy, I'm not saying you don't need to be careful, but in my experience, it's a cowardly person who leaves an anonymous note like that. You can't control or take responsibility for someone else's bad behavior. And, besides, we're the ones who are supposed to take care of you, and not the other way around. Don't waste your time worrying about us; let us worry about you," Mr. Middleton said. "We're old, and we don't have much else to do. Don't take away our one hobby."

Lacy laughed, thinking again how glad she was that he had come into her life. "All right. I didn't really want to move anyway," she admitted. Lucinda smiled and stood to retrieve another cinnamon roll for Lacy, her third, but Lacy stopped her.

"They're delicious, Grandma, but I really can't. I have a meeting this morning."

"You be careful," Lucinda admonished. "I don't like this business at all, Lacy."

"Neither do I, Grandma." She stood and kissed her grandparents goodbye before walking to her grandmother's car. Anger fueled her steps, and she wished that she could walk to town, not only to burn off some calories, but to burn off some of her frustration as well. How dare someone vandalize her grandmother's house?

She was a block away from home when she noticed the car following in her rearview mirror. All of her anger and righteous indignation returned and then exploded into something irrational. Instead of heading toward town and the mayor's office, Lacy turned and headed out into the country. The car, of course, followed.

Once she was a reasonable distance from town, she attempted Keegan's maneuver from the day before by speeding up, slamming her foot on the brake, and jerking the wheel a hard left. Her car fishtailed and careened a few feet, but finally she had it back on track. Instead of maintaining her lane to pass the car that had been following her, she got in the opposite lane and played a game of chicken, forcing the car to come to a screeching halt.

Lacy in a temper was a very bad thing because she lost all rational thought, including the possibility that the person in the car may be armed and dangerous. Instead of stalling and calling the police like a sane person, she erupted from her car and advanced on the driver's side, jerking open the door and poking her head inside. There she saw a pale, trembling teenager with his hands clenched on the wheel. Beside him sat a paunchy, middle-aged man who looked equally as petrified.

"I don't have any money, lady," the kid said.

Lacy looked down at the open door in her hand and read the emblem on the side. "A-1 Driving School." *Uh-oh.* "I'm so sorry," Lacy said. She gently closed the door and took a nonthreatening step away. "I thought you were someone else."

The kid nodded, still staring straight ahead as if afraid to make eye contact.

"Really," Lacy began, trying to explain again, but her phone rang. She held up a finger for the kid to wait—the least she could do was give him some money—and pulled out her phone. It was Travis.

"The ballistics test came back this morning." He was whispering, so she knew he was at work.

"What did it say?" For whatever reason, she whispered, too.

"It's a match, Lacy."

"What?" this time she yelled. Beside her, the kid and the middle-aged man jumped in terror.

"Drive, Andy, just drive," the older man yelled as he gripped the dashboard. The kid, Andy, stomped his foot on the pedal and sped away, leaving Lacy standing in the middle of the road with her phone still pressed to her ear in shock.

* * *

Somehow, Lacy made it to the mayor's office only a minute late. Perhaps she had sped. She didn't remember. All she knew was that she had been in a stupor after Travis's impossible announcement. How could the ballistics have been a match?

He couldn't tell her, both because he didn't know and because he wasn't able to talk just then. They had disconnected and Lacy had gotten in her car to try and make her meeting.

Now she was in the mayor's lobby, and some of the numbness was starting to wear away. Obviously there had been some sort of monumental error somewhere along the line. She would talk to Jason today and ask him how the mixup had occurred. Maybe ballistics tests weren't as reliable as she thought. After all, lie detector tests had been repeatedly proved unreliable; maybe it was the same thing with ballistics.

Whatever the reason, she tried to force her mind to focus on what she needed to ask the mayor. When she was at last called into his inner sanctum, she realized he thought she was there to discuss the Stakely building.

"Well, Lacy, hello," he said. He stood and leaned over his desk to shake her hand. "I had hoped you would come to your senses about that old monstrosity of a building. The good news is that the developers still want it, and they're willing to pay exactly what you paid for it, so you won't lose any money."

Lacy blinked at him in confusion for a minute. He thought she was here to sell her building? "I'm not selling the Stakely building. I'm going to renovate." She sank weakly into the proffered chair, and he did the same on the other side of the desk.

"Not selling? But I thought that was why you were here today."

"No, I came to talk to you about something that happened in the Stakely building a long time ago."

The mayor pulled out a handkerchief and dabbed at his upper lip. "I can't imagine what you might be talking about."

"The Susan Pendergast murder."

"That's an unpleasant topic I prefer not to revisit." Dab, dab, dab.

"I realize it's an unpleasant topic, and I am sorry to rehash it, but in light of current events, I really feel it's important."

"What current events?" He moved on to dabbing his forehead. If the conversation went on a long time, would he lift his elbow and dab at his armpits?

"Ed McNeil's murder."

"I don't see how the two are connected," the mayor said. He turned on a small fan and pointed it at his face. The humming noise was distracting, but Lacy was undeterred.

"I'm not sure I do, either, but there are too many coincidences to ignore. For instance, you."

"Me?" the mayor said. He pointed at himself in case Lacy had made some mistake.

"You were a suspect in the original murder."

"Now, see here, I was never a suspect. Susan and I were engaged, true, but things were going well."

"Even though you cheated on her with her sister?" It was a shot in the dark, but apparently a correct one.

"Who told you about that? Did Sheila tell you that? Because she's lying." He gripped the edge of his desk and leaned forward, his face turning an ugly shade of puce.

"I really don't care about that," Lacy lied. In truth, she was deeply curious about it, but she had bigger fish to fry today. "My only interest here is in trying to figure out how these two cases are related and what they have to do with the Stakely building."

"Nothing. There's nothing suspicious about the Stakely building. Nothing at all." Dab, dab, dab.

"Then why have I received two threatening messages? Why has a car been following me?"

"I really don't know," the mayor said. He picked up his phone and pressed a button. "Is my nine o'clock here yet?"

Lacy figured that was code for "Get me a nine o'clock, stat!" but still she persisted. "If you'll just help me and answer a few of my questions, then I'll go away."

"I really don't have time for this, Miss Steele," he replied. He looked down and straightened some papers on his desk. Lacy noted that his hands were trembling. He cleared his throat and looked up, but his focus rested just slightly to the right of her eyes. "There's no connection between Ed McNeil and Susan. The two cases are unrelated. There is no connection to the Stakely building." His voice quavered and cracked on the word "Stakely," and he cleared his throat. "Now, if you'll please excuse me, I have to get back to the business of running this town."

"Fine," Lacy said, standing. "But let me tell you that I own the Stakely building now with no intention of selling it. In fact, I plan to go over it with a fine-tooth comb until I figure out what is going on. I have the money and the time to do exactly as I've promised, and I have a connection to the paper that ensures anything I find will come to light. If you think I'm going to give up and let this go, then you are sadly mistaken. Thank you for your time today."

She turned to go, thinking the meeting was over, but the mayor called out to her. "Wait," he choked. Lacy turned around in time to see him mop his entire face with the handkerchief. "I am telling you for your own good to let this go. Let the past stay buried and move on with your future. The building is too much for a young girl like you, and you don't want to get involved in the politics in this town. Believe me. Just let it go."

Lacy tried to figure out if his concern was for her or for himself, but she couldn't tell. "Maybe that would be possible if someone hadn't involved my friends and family in this mess. Now it's too late. I'm seeing this through until the end."

"You've been warned," the mayor said. Lacy watched as he swiped his face once more, and then she turned and let herself out.

CHAPTER 16

Keegan volunteered to go to the Joe Anton interview with Lacy. "He's a convicted criminal. I don't feel comfortable about letting you talk to him alone," was his reason. Lacy wondered if he was simply curious. She took her grandmother's car back to her house where Keegan was waiting and they drove to the jail together.

Lacy expected to have to wait a long time for Mr. Anton to arrive, but Travis had worked his magic so the man was actually waiting on them when they entered the visitation room.

He was as small and frail as Lacy remembered, with lanky white hair slicked back from his head. His pallor was a sickly white, his watery brown eyes not quite focused, and his face covered with a not-so-fine layer of stubble. One side of his lip drooped and drooled a constant stream of saliva. Lacy forced herself not to stare at it.

"Thank you for seeing us today, Mr. Anton," Lacy said as they sat down. The man nodded, and she continued. "I'm sure you know why I'm here. I have some questions about the murder all those years ago."

"I dunno what help I'll be. I barely remember what I had for breakfast this morning." His hands trembled as he placed them in his lap, but, unlike the mayor, Lacy didn't think it was from nerves. His body seemed worn out by so much drug use.

"Is it all right if we go over the facts of the case?" she asked. Her tone was naturally gentle with him because, even though he was a convicted murderer, he seemed small and helpless somehow. He nodded, and she continued. "The article I read said that you had a drug supplier who worked in the area of the Stakely building. Is that true?"

He nodded again. She wasn't going to get much from him if all he did was nod, but this time he added words. "Yeah, but I hung out there because I liked it, too. There were lots of people and pretty things. I liked to look at the artwork."

"You argued with Susan Pendergast shortly before her murder."

"I don't know if I remember this part, or if people have told me about it, but I seem to recall arguing with her. She was upset 'cause I was high again. She saw me hanging around the parking lot, shooting up, and she told me to go away." He frowned, squinting as he tried to see through the fog of his memory. "No, that's not right—she told me to go and get help, but she said it angry-like. I think maybe she was a do-gooder, but she was a large, powerful woman and everyone assumed she was angry 'cause she was loud."

Having met Sheila and seen her forceful personality up close, Lacy thought he was probably correct.

"Had you ever talked to Susan before?"

He nodded again. "I wouldn't say we were friends because, truth be told, I was kind of scared of her. She was like a teacher I had once—strict and intimidating. But she was nice underneath it all. Sometimes she nodded at me or let me sit in her store when I was too stoned to be out walking around."

"Did you ever see her sister, Sheila Whitaker, or the mayor, Hal Watkins?"

When he shook his head, Lacy was disappointed, but then he spoke. "I don't remember, but I must have because after the police questioned me the first time, I told my sister about a fight I saw between the three of them."

"You saw Susan, Sheila, and the mayor fighting with each other?" Lacy repeated. "What were they fighting about?"

"I don't remember, but, according to what I told my sister, it was pretty bad. Susan slapped Sheila and Sheila punched her in the face. The mayor tried to intervene, and they both turned on him. Apparently it was a real cat fight." He smiled with the good side of his mouth. "I kind of wish I could remember it."

"Why did this information never come to trial?" The article had only said that they argued and never that Susan had told him to get help. "Did you ever tell your lawyer?"

Mr. Anton nodded. "I told him a few times, and my sister volunteered to testify about what I'd told her, but Mr. McNeil said it wasn't important."

Lacy was quiet a few beats while she processed that, but Mr. Anton didn't seem to notice. He turned to stare at the opposite wall, apparently lost in a daydream. If what he said was true, then Ed McNeil was either the world's worst lawyer or purposely incompetent. The prosecution had alleged that Joe Anton's motive for murder was revenge for their argument, but if Susan had simply been urging the man to get help, then there had been no argument and there was no motive. And if there had been a physical altercation involving Sheila and the mayor then that gave both of them motive. "Mr. Anton, are you sure you told Ed McNeil what you just told me, that Susan wasn't angry and was trying to urge you to get help? Are you sure you told him about the argument between Susan, Sheila, and Hal Watkins?"

Mr. Anton nodded vigorously as droplets of spittle flew off his chin. "I told him back then, and I told him this time, too. He said it wasn't important."

The information was monumental, but Lacy didn't have time to dwell on it right now. "Your alibi was what eventually led to your arrest. When you were interviewed at the time of the murder, you said you were at the races all day at the track a couple of hours away. Why do you think the officers at the time believed you?"

"Because I gave them a copy of my ticket stub, or at least I thought I did. I meant to. Maybe I dreamed it because when they opened the file and looked again, it was gone. There was no copy of the ticket and no mention of me giving them a stub. I really thought I did that, but sometimes I dream things, and I think they're real. Maybe I wasn't even at the track that day. I don't know. All I know is that I never killed anybody. I might be a user and a drunk, but I've never been a violent one." He shifted in his seat and leaned forward. "I went to court-ordered drug counseling once, and the therapist said that I was non-violent on drugs that usually make people violent. She seemed to think that was a big deal, and wanted to test my brain to see if my chemicals were off."

"There's a record of a professional stating that you're non-violent?" Lacy clarified.

Mr. Anton nodded.

"Did you tell this information to Mr. McNeil?"

The man nodded again. "At least I think I did. Sometimes I'm not sure what's real and what's not. Like right now I might be dreaming. Pretty girls don't ever come visit me. That seems like something I might make up." He narrowed his eyes at Lacy and peered closer, touching his nose to the glass as he made his inspection.

"I'm real," she told him.

"That's what the dreams always say. It's very confusing."

"Real or dream, I'm trying to help you," Lacy said. "Do you believe that?"

He shrugged. "It doesn't really matter. Mr. McNeil said he was going to get me out this time, and look how that turned out."

"Do you know anyone who might have wanted to frame you? Do you know anything that might have led to Susan's death or Ed McNeil's death?" Lacy pressed.

"No, and if I did, it's long forgotten. But I don't think I ever did. I'm not exactly the person people tell their secrets to. I know it wasn't much, but I lived a quiet little life getting high, and that was all. Sometimes I stole things to get money, but I never hurt anyone. I've never even thrown a punch. I just wanted to be left alone to enjoy my drugs, and that's all I want now." He looked furtively around the room. "Not that I'm on drugs now, because I'm not."

Lacy had her doubts about that; she knew it wasn't unheard of for criminals to have access to drugs in prison. At the very least, they had access to prescription drugs. "Thank you for your time, Mr. Anton. I want you to know I'm looking into your case, as well as the murder of Ed McNeil. In my opinion, two men stand accused of murders they didn't commit, and if I'm correct, then I think the same person committed both murders."

"I'm not sure I understand what you just said, but it sounds like you don't think the cop killed my lawyer. Don't believe it, though. All cops are crooked."

"Just like all druggies are murderers," she said.

He opened his mouth to reply and left it hanging. "You just blew my mind," he said.

She couldn't help but laugh at his earnest tone. "That's only fair because you've blown my mind today, too. Thank you for your help and your time."

"What else do I have to do with my time?" he said, but he was smiling as he stood and shuffled away.

Lacy turned to Keegan who had remained quiet and observant throughout the interview. "What do you think?" she asked. Were his impressions and conclusions as monumental as hers?

"Maybe I'm a bleeding heart, but I don't think he did it. And it sounds like this Ed McNeil suppressed vital information that could have led to his acquittal."

"That's what I think, too. The question is why? Why would Ed McNeil take his case and do such a poor job with it, not just once, but twice? According to Sheila, he passionately believed Joe was innocent and wanted to get him out, but according to Joe, he put up a lackluster defense that was so full of holes it was no wonder the man was convicted. I don't get Ed McNeil's angle. Was he trying to protect someone? Sheila, maybe, or possibly the mayor? Why did he contribute to the SAD and put a stop-work order on my place? Why was he playing both sides of the fence on so many issues? Sheila painted him as some selfless individual, and his secretary, Pearl, was wholly devoted, but I don't think Ed McNeil ever did anything that wasn't for his own personal gain. But what did he have to gain by all this? I feel like if we could figure that out, then we might understand why he was murdered and who did it."

"Any ideas on how to figure that out?" Keegan asked.

"None whatsoever, but I think we discovered a new lead."

"We did? What is it?"

"Mr. Anton said he told his sister everything. According to the article on the old case, she's still alive and still his main support. Let's see if we can talk to her."

"This is so cool," Keegan said, smiling like an eager little boy as they left the jail. "We're like *Cagney and Lacey*, that old show. *Keegan and Lacy*. We need a theme song."

"There's an ancient Justin Bieber CD floating around in my bedroom somewhere. Maybe we could find something on that."

He surprised her by singing a shockingly good rendition of "Baby," Justin Bieber's breakout song, smiling when Lacy giggled in delight.

"That was unexpectedly amazing," she said, linking her arm with his. "So you're a secret Bieber fan. Did not see that coming."

"Nah, but that song was gold when I was a kid. Girls loved it. Still do, apparently," he said, tossing her an exaggerated wink that made her laugh again.

"You've always been a lady's man, huh?" she guessed. He would have been like Jason, forever suave, never awkward like her and Tosh.

"Totally and completely," he said. His face lost some of its humor as momentary sadness or seriousness settled over it. When he realized she was studying him, he shook off the melancholy and plastered on a smile again. "Do you know where this lady lives?"

"Does Inspector Poirot ever go into a case without knowledge?" she asked, pressing her hand to her chest in mock affront.

"You have no idea, do you?" he said.

"None whatsoever, but it shouldn't be too hard to find. You know what I think this outing needs?"

"What?" he asked, leaning closer in gleeful expectation, as if he sensed shenanigans afoot.

"A little more Underwood. What do you say we stop by and see if we can coax Tosh to come out and play?"

"I'd say you're good for what ails all the Underwoods," he said, pausing to open the car door for her before tucking her safely inside.

CHAPTER 17

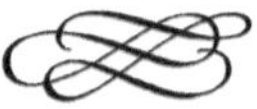

Lacy decided not to let herself read anything into Tosh's suspicious silence the last few days. After all, he was insanely busy since his secretary retired. Maybe he was genuinely busy. Maybe Lacy needed to put extra effort into tracking him down. Maybe he would appreciate being kidnapped to participate in their hijinks. Maybe she was grasping at straws in every area of life now.

"Aren't you coming?" Lacy asked Keegan when they arrived at Tosh's church and he made no move to leave the car.

"I think it will go better if you go alone," he said.

"You and Tosh aren't fighting, are you?" she asked.

"No more than usual," he said, reaching for his book as she slid from the car.

The church was always a bit spooky when it was deserted. She wasn't alone in thinking that. Tosh admitted he had also been a little creeped out without the presence of his secretary to fill the place with noise. "Tosh," she called, her voice echoing cavernously in the narthex. The scene was reminiscent of her early morning discovery of Ed McNeil's body, so much that her hands tensed, gripping into fists at her sides. *Keep walking, Tosh is fine,* she assured herself. After all, the list of people who wanted him dead was empty, unlike the smarmy Ed McNeil.

A strange sound bounced out of Tosh's office, trundling down the hallway to greet her. It almost sounded like the barking of a dog, but Tosh didn't have a dog and bringing one to church didn't seem like something he would do. Anxiety lodged is Lacy's throat as she followed the sound. She palmed her phone, but she had no idea who to call. If something was terribly wrong, if Tosh was in trouble, where would she turn? It wasn't until that moment she realized how much she had come to rely on Jason. It wasn't that she called him constantly or even reached out when she was in trouble. It was that she felt like she could. Somehow in an impossibly short amount of time he had come to represent backup for her, to give her a measure of internal security in an insecure world. That thought was so terrifying she refused to dwell on it. Jason was not responsible for her, was not in charge of taking care of her. She was a grown woman who did that on her own. She told herself as much over and over as she made herself move toward the strange barking sound in Tosh's office.

When she finally reached it she stopped short, trying to assimilate the strange scene. The barking sound at least had a reference point because it wasn't coming from a dog; it was coming from a woman, a large woman in Tosh's arms.

Pearl, Ed McNeil's land barge of a secretary, was wetting Tosh's shirt with copious amounts of tears. The barking sound was coming from her and, if she weren't so disconcerted, Lacy might have giggled. She had no idea humans could sound like injured seals when they wept. Tosh looked pained, either because his ears hurt from being assaulted with Pearl's yapping howls of grief or because she put her full weigh on him as she did so. Right now he looked like Sisyphus must have as he attempted to roll the giant boulder uphill. He was putting everything he had into keeping a weeping Pearl upright, but soon it might not be enough. Soon she might collapse onto him like a dying star, and then what?

Lacy stood in the doorway watching them unobserved, uncertain of what to do. Tosh looked like he needed a rescue from Pearl's desperate and crushing grief, but Lacy wasn't certain she was the one who should provide it. Last time she and Pearl met up, things hadn't gone well. *Keegan.* She remembered him sitting in the car like a gift. She would retrieve him and send him to try and free Tosh from Pearl's piercing, tear-filled clutches. He would do it with so much charm Pearl wouldn't realize she was being handled. But when she turned to go, the movement caught the attention of the inhabitants of the room.

"Lacy," Tosh said, sounding both relieved and distressed, but it was Pearl who commanded her notice.

"You," she said, grief switching to rage with seemingly no in between. She let go of Tosh with a little shove that sent him tumbling backward a step and then rounded on Lacy, arms outstretched in a manner that was becoming familiar. For a few beats she blinked at the menacing, advancing woman, frozen in terror.

"*Go,*" Tosh shouted, and she came to her senses, turning to dash down the hallway as if running for her life, as she most assuredly was. If Pearl caught her, she could do a lot of damage, whether she meant to or not. Lacy was much more petite and even when Pearl wasn't filled with irrational ire she could probably twist Lacy into a pretzel with her hands. Now, though, filled with so much homicidal angst, she could probably snap her neck without breaking a sweat.

"Pearl, wait, stop," Tosh called, bringing up the rear as he chased Pearl, who was busy chasing Lacy. Lacy didn't pause to see if his words had any effect. She ran for her life, sprinting toward Keegan's car as Pearl's heavy footsteps pounded behind her. How did someone run so fast in compression socks and orthopedic loafers? Yet somehow Pearl did.

Lacy burst into the sunlight. Her mind had the sudden and wild thought that maybe she was free now. Maybe Pearl would evaporate in the sunlight, like a vampire, but she knew that wasn't true because Pearl had already chased her into the sun the last time she tried to kill her. So she didn't stop running, not until she reached Keegan's car, fumbled for the handle, and tossed herself inside.

Keegan eyed her in silence as she fumbled, first for the lock and then for her seatbelt.

"Drive," she commanded in a shaky pant, squinting toward Tosh's church for any sings of Pearl. There were none. Either Tosh was able to subdue her or Lacy was faster than she thought and had merely outrun her. She had no plans to stick around and see what happened next. The more distance she put between herself and the psychotic woman, the better.

Keegan started the car and put it into gear, not saying a word until they were a few blocks from the church. Then he leaned over and gave her knee a pat. "Best distraction ever."

Lacy couldn't answer; she was still trying to get her breath back and calm the panicked flapping of her heart.

* * *

Marilyn Anton lived in a quiet neighborhood a couple of streets away from Barbara Blake's house. The proximity was nothing unusual; the town was so small everything was a few blocks from everywhere. The nicest neighborhood in town was the Victorian section downtown, old formerly painted ladies who had fallen into blatant neglect and disrepair over the decades. Many had been broken up into smaller rental units. Some, Lacy suspected, were becoming drug hideouts. *Maybe someday I'll renovate those, too,* she thought and then quickly checked herself. What was she talking about? She was barely twenty six. It wasn't her mission in life to singlehandedly renovate her entire hometown. Was it?

Outside of the grand Victorian manors, most houses in town were post-war bungalows like Barbara Blake's. Also like Marilyn Anton's. She greeted them with a wary expression, hand gripping the door for support. Obviously she knew they were there to ask about her brother's case, but she had no way of knowing if they were friend or foe. Did they think Joe was innocent or were they planning to use him in some way? What must it be like to be an adult and still be your brother's keeper? Lacy couldn't imagine, especially because she was currently not speaking to her only sibling.

"Hello, Miss Anton. I'm Lacy Steele, we spoke a moment ago on the phone. I'm a reporter for the local paper, but that's not why I'm here. I wanted to talk to you about your brother's case."

"What about it?" Despite her reticence, her voice was soft and gentle. Clearly she was a woman with a big and tender heart, one that had probably been put through a meat grinder over the years since her brother's arrest.

"Some inconsistencies in his case have come to light, and I wanted to ask you about them," Lacy said.

Marilyn blinked at her as if trying to take her measure and come to a decision. At last she opened the door wider and stepped back. "Please come in."

They followed her to the living room. She sheepishly removed a pile of clean laundry from the couch so they could sit down. "Sorry," she muttered.

"Please don't apologize. We gave you no warning," Lacy said.

"You have a lovely home," Keegan said with such warm sincerity Marilyn was immediately at ease.

"Thank you," she said. "You had questions about Joe?"

Lacy took a breath and began. "The truth is, Ms. Anton, I have no idea if your brother killed Susan Pendergast, but I'm beginning to have grave doubts. At the very least I think his entire case has been badly mishandled from the beginning. What was your opinion of Ed McNeil?"

She watched as a familiar light of softness eased over Marilyn's features. "Oh, Ed was wonderful."

I threw up in my mouth a little, Lacy thought. What on earth kind of mojo had Ed McNeil possessed that he tricked all middle aged women into believing he was a catch? Did people lose good taste and common sense as they aged? *Something to look out for in my future.* "What makes you say that?" If it sounded like she was choking on a pinecone, it couldn't be helped. Ed McNeil, wonderful. *Nope.*

"He took on Joe's case pro bono. Twice."

"He worked for free? Both times?"

Marilyn nodded. "That was the kind of man he was, selfless."

Lacy decided not to poke at that statement. "I spoke with your brother today."

"You did?" Marilyn said, sounding shocked.

"Why does that surprise you?" Lacy asked. The best way to get to the bottom of things was to go directly to the source, in her opinion.

"People tend to overlook Joe, they always have. First because they thought he was a worthless druggie, and then because he's a worthless murderer. But neither has ever been true. Joe is sweet, warm, and gentle. He would never hurt anyone for any reason."

"Even when he was high?" Lacy prodded.

Marilyn shook her head. "Look, I'm not saying drugs are good or that I approve of them, please don't misunderstand me. I wish my brother had never gotten addicted. It's taken a terrible toll on our family, clearly. But he wasn't like those people you see on TV who go all wild and crazy and violent. He sort of went into a stupor and stared into space. I lost my brother to drugs, but it was a quiet and peaceful passing, if you know what I mean. They took over his life, but in a nonviolent way."

Lacy thought she did know. The more she learned about Joe Anton, the more she had the sense he had been unfairly judged and dismissed as a worthless lost cause. And she began to wonder if someone had used him as a pawn to take the fall for a heinous crime he didn't commit.

"Can you take me back to that time, please? What do you know about what happened? Start with the Stakely building."

She sighed. "Joe's always loved that old place. We used to go there when we were kids, we'd bike to town and buy a pickle or candy. Those were good days, when the market was bustling, right along with the town. He kind of fixated on it, I think, as a representation of everything right in our world. Our parents didn't always get along, there was a lot of tension in our home, and the Stakely building became a kind of escape for him, emotional and otherwise. When he was a teen, some bad apples began hanging out there and he got sucked in." She frowned as if remembering something unpleasant.

"Does Joe still keep in contact with those people?"

She gave a humorless chuckle. "No. One bad apple reformed in a major way."

Lacy tensed expectantly. Marilyn's tone told her she was about to hear something that would change the game completely. "What do you mean?"

"Everyone knew my brother was on drugs. No one ever asked where he got them."

"Do you know who his supplier was?"

"Absolutely I do," Marilyn said, tone going hard with anger. "It was the mayor's son, the man who is now our current mayor."

Lacy blinked at her a few times, processing. "The mayor was a drug dealer?"

Marilyn nodded. "Small time. He was cocky and liked the status of being a secret rebel. His daddy kept him on a short leash. He enjoyed the panache of selling dope, of making a few extra bucks to spend on his girl. *Girls*, he was seeing both sisters."

"Wow," Lacy said. Somehow she thought all old people were good, that drugs and crime were something reserved for her generation. Apparently not. Apparently love triangles and drugs and murder had been going on forever. She took a breath and forced herself to ask the next question. "Do you think the mayor killed Susan?"

Now it was Marilyn's turn to take a breath and pause. "Not really. Don't get me wrong, I think he's a weasel. He was a punk then, and he's a punk now. He might not deal dope anymore, but I'm sure if you poked around a little he still has his finger in a few illegal pies. But he was also a coward of the first order. I can't imagine him picking up a gun, let alone shooting it with intent to kill one of his girlfriends. He's more the type that would hire someone else to do it."

"If you don't think he did it, who do you think killed Susan?" Lacy asked.

Marilyn shrugged. "A lot of bad apples hung around the Stakely building in those days. And, as I said, the mayor was a peon. Somewhere he had a higher up, a bigger boss who supplied the drugs. Maybe that person was trying to send a message. I'm not certain we'll ever know who did it, but I know who didn't. There is absolutely no way my brother murdered anyone."

Somehow, Lacy believed her. Maybe because it was the same way she was certain Jason didn't murder Ed McNeil.

"I believe you," she declared, offering Marilyn a smile. "And I'm going to do everything in my power to prove it." The two women shared a smile of understanding. They shook hands as if sealing an oath, and Lacy followed Keegan to the car.

CHAPTER 18

"Are you humming the theme to *Mission Impossible*?" Lacy asked Keegan once they were safely buckled into his car.

"Too much?" he asked, quirking an eyebrow at her.

"No, I like it," she said, tossing him a smile.

"Where to next, Sherlock?"

"You are stuffed to the gills with old timey detective references," she noted.

"The classics never go out of style," he said.

"In answer to your question, I need to go back to the jail and speak with Jason before visiting hours end. But I must reiterate that you do not have to drive me places. Please don't feel like you need to be my chauffer if you have something better to do."

"What could possibly be better than playing Jeeves to your Wooster?" he asked.

"I don't even know that one."

He clucked disapprovingly at her. "What? You've never read P.G. Wodehouse? I'll send you one."

"You're all kinds of spectacular," she said earnestly, studying his profile. He was a fascinating mystery, one she neither had time nor energy to decipher. The best part was that he was so pleasant to look at and be around while she made the attempt. An attractive man who expected absolutely nothing from her—was anything in life better than that?

Soon they arrived at the jail and she asked to see an attractive man who *did* expect things from her. What things, she had no idea. But she knew they were presently beyond her capacity to bestow. And yet still she came back for more.

Keegan walked her inside, remaining on vigil like a protective servant until the heavy metal door clanged to announce Jason's arrival. "I'll leave you alone now," he said cheerfully. He nodded at Jason as he made his way out of the visitation room.

Jason sat, looking tired and grumpy as he picked up the phone. "Looks like things are going well between you two. When's the wedding?"

He was spoiling for an argument, but Lacy wasn't about to give him one by rising to take the bait. "How are you?"

"I'm pretty sure you know the answer to that question, Red. My lawyer wants me to take a plea."

Lacy sat forward so abruptly her chair darted backwards and she had to grab the edge of the table to keep from falling off. "What?" She reached down and righted her chair with her free hand. "Jason, that's insane. You can't plead for something you didn't do."

There was a pause before he spoke again. "You don't think I did it?"

"Are you crazy? You even have to ask me that question? I know you didn't do it. Don't be ridiculous."

"But the ballistics..." he trailed off and turned to look at the wall, blinking furiously a few times. Lacy wondered if he was trying to compose himself.

"The ballistics are wrong. Or something else is wrong. Actually everything is wrong at the moment, with you in here. I don't know what it is, but I'm going to figure it out."

He looked back at her again, and he was frowning this time. "The ballistics are never wrong. They're like fingerprints. Each gun leaves its own striations on the bullet."

"Who had access to your gun?"

"No one. It's either on me or locked in my desk at home at all times. No one touched it, no one broke into my house. Nothing." He shook his head and swiped his hand wearily over his face. "This is impossible."

"I'm going to talk to the person who did the ballistics test and find out how this mistake happened. And then I'm going to talk to everyone I can find to figure out how such a monumental mix up might have occurred. There has to be some reasonable explanation."

"No," Jason said, his tone vehement now. "Why won't you listen to me when I tell you to stay out of it? It's like beating my head against a brick. I don't want you talking to anyone in forensics, I don't want you talking to Joe Anton, I don't want you sticking your nose into places that might get you killed. Do you have any idea what it's doing to me to know you're out there unprotected while I'm stuck in here?"

"Do you have any idea what it's doing to me to know you're in here without me while I'm stuck out there?"

"That's not the same, not at all. That's so...you're so..." He broke off and took a deep breath, swallowing hard as he gripped the phone tighter. "Can you listen to reason for once and stop this madness?"

She stared at him through the glass divider, shaking her head slowly as she mouthed the word, "*No.*"

His scowl turned impressively dark and scary, though no less sexy. He could be the next cover model for a *Prisoners Gone Wild* calendar. Lacy was certain the overhead fluorescent lights made her look wan and pasty, casting her skin with an unhealthy yellow glow. On Jason they pleasantly highlighted all the angles of his face, as if he were shooting a gritty prison drama for an artsy filmmaker. "If you insist on pursuing this matter further, then don't come back because I won't see you."

She stared at him, trying to gauge his motivation. She had no doubt he was serious; if she kept investigating, he would refuse to see her when she tried to visit. What she couldn't figure out was whether or not he was trying to protect her or himself. Was he trying to cut her off because he thought he was going to spend the rest of his life in jail and he didn't want her hanging on?

"If that's how you want to play it, then fine. Refuse my visit. But I think you know me well enough by now to realize I'm not giving up until this thing is finished, one way or another."

"Lacy, doesn't it occur to you that it might finish with your death?"

"Then at least people would know you're innocent."

She jumped when he pulled the phone away from his ear and banged it on the counter a few times in frustration. "Woman, you are making me crazy," he yelled when he put it back to his face.

"Welcome to my world," she yelled, purposely lowering her tone when one of the jailers poked his head into the room to check on them. She pictured the type of people who usually visited the jail and wondered if anyone had ever had a screaming match with their significant other or family member before.

"Fine, martyr, you don't care about you, but what about your new BFF? Aren't you worried all these hornet nests you're poking are going to have an effect on him? If the pastor's brother is learning what you're learning, then doesn't it stand to reason that they're going to go after him, too?"

"Keegan is going back to Chicago in a couple of days. He'll be fine."

"Then they'll go after the pastor."

Now it was Lacy's turn to swallow down her emotions. "Tosh isn't speaking to me right now."

Jason frowned. "Why not?"

"I don't know," she said, and to her embarrassment her voice quavered.

"Jerk," Jason said, probably knowing it would make Lacy laugh, which it did. They smiled, enjoying a peaceful interlude from their heated exchange.

"When you get out of here, maybe I'll let you beat him up," Lacy said.

Jason laughed and shook his head. "Now I know you think I'm never getting out."

"I don't think that," Lacy said seriously. "And if your lawyer thinks that, then fire him and hire another one. Or I'll find you one. You know I'm rich now. I could probably get that guy who got OJ off."

"I'm pretty sure he's dead, but thanks. Or rather, no thanks. I'll stick with my lawyer and we'll decide together how it's going to pan out."

"Jason, please don't admit to something you didn't do."

"You know you're the only person who's sure I didn't do it. Why is that?"

"Maybe I'm the only person who really knows you," Lacy suggested.

"Maybe so," Jason said. He glanced at the clock on the wall and Lacy noted their allotted visitation time was almost at an end. "Lacy, would it help if I begged you to let things go?"

"No."

He sighed. "That's pretty much what I thought you'd say." He took a breath, shoring himself up. "Fine. I meant what I said. If you're intent on doing this, then don't come back. I won't see you."

"Fine," Lacy said, trying not to show how deeply his words hurt. "I guess this is goodbye, then, because I won't stop until this is over."

"Eventually you'll give up and lose interest," he said.

"If you think that, you don't know me at all," she said.

They maintained eye contact for a few beats until he finally broke away.

"I guess this is goodbye. Take care of you, Red," he said. Without looking at her or waiting for an answer, he hung up and turned his back as he stood waiting for the door to open. Lacy remained frozen, watching until the heavy metal door swallowed him up, trying not to drown in hopelessness. Then she calmly hung up the phone, stood, and walked out of the jail. Instead of pausing in the lobby to talk to Keegan, she went to the sheriff's office and pushed the intercom button, doing the one thing she had promised herself she would never do again. Taking a deep breath, she opened her mouth and forced out the painful words.

"Lacy Steele to see Detective Brenner, please."

CHAPTER 19

Lacy wasn't sure if Detective Brenner would agree to see her, but he must have been able to smell crow a mile away.

"Lacy," he said as she was led into his office. "This is a surprise, especially in light of—what did you call it—my 'complete and utter incompetence.'"

Lacy sat and swallowed her pride. "Let's be grownups about this. I will admit I shouldn't have handled my complaints in a public forum, if you will admit you mishandled my grandmother's case."

"I wasn't aware apologies came with qualifiers," he replied.

They glared at each other over his desk in a silent standoff, seeing who would blink first. Finally he capitulated.

"Fine, mistakes were made in your grandmother's case."

Lacy nodded, willing to let the past go, especially in light of present circumstances. "I came here today because I need your help. Please."

"I assume you're referring to Jason's situation."

"Yes. I need to know how the mistake with the ballistics occurred."

"What mistake?" he asked, confused.

"I don't know—whatever mistake indicated a match. Admittedly

I'm not much of an expert on these things, but there has to be some margin of error."

"I *am* an expert on these matters, at least enough to know when there's been no mistake. Did you know our state uses ALIAS? That's a 3-D imaging system for ballistics matching, and there is no margin of error."

"But," she tried again, and he held up a hand to interrupt.

"Look, Lacy, this is hard for all of us. None of us wanted to believe Jason was guilty. Taking him into custody was a necessary evil. We all thought he would be out as soon as the test came back, but the forensics don't lie. There's just no other explanation."

She wanted to be angry with him, but he wasn't being his usual bombastic self. Instead he sounded sincere and sympathetic.

"I think this case is related to the Susan Pendergast case," Lacy blurted, hoping to she hadn't made a monumental error in judgment by trusting him.

"Of course it is. Jason is the arresting officer, and Ed McNeil was the attorney."

"No, I mean besides the obvious connection. I think the same person killed both Susan and Ed."

He sighed. "Lacy, that's not possible." His tone was a mixture of exasperation and pity.

"I know it's not probable, but it is possible. What if the same person who killed them also framed Jason? This is all tied up with the Stakely building somehow, too."

"The Stakely building? What does that have to do with anything?" He was back to looking baffled.

"I bought the Stakely building, where the original murder took place, and suddenly I'm receiving threats and being followed. The same players who are involved now were involved then. I don't know why or how, but things are connected."

"I'll admit there's some coincidence there, but I think that's all it is," he said.

"But there has to be some way to prove a connection." She leaned forward. "The bullet from the Pendergast murder was never recovered. What if I find it while I'm renovating? Could you run it and see if it came from the same gun that killed Ed McNeil?"

He shook his head. "The gun that killed Ed McNeil's is Jason's."

"Could you run it anyway? I mean if this 3D system is such a big deal, then maybe it can tell us a lot of information about where the bullet came from." She knew she sounded desperate; she *was* desperate.

"Fine. If, in the one in a million chance that you find a bullet that's been missing for almost a quarter of a century, then I will run it." He folded his hands on his desk and leaned forward. "I'm going to level with you. I don't like civilians interfering with my cases, and I like reporters even less. I'm tolerating you because of your relationship with Jason. He's a good kid, and he was a good officer. But you're in over your head here, and you're grasping at straws."

"I don't disagree with anything you said. I have no idea what I'm doing. All I know is that Jason did not kill Ed McNeil. You said yourself he's a good man and a good officer."

"Good people do bad things every day," he said.

She shook her head. "No. There is nothing anyone could say to change my mind. If I have to tear the Stakely building apart with my bare hands to find some more evidence from the Pendergast case, then that's what I'll do. Also, I think the mayor did it." She slapped her hand over her mouth. She hadn't meant to impart that last tidbit during her impassioned speech.

"The mayor?" Detective Brenner roared, sitting back so quickly in his chair it groaned. "You cannot go around accusing public officials with no proof. That's slander."

"You're probably right about all of that, too, but he was in a love triangle with Susan and Sheila all those years ago, and he was in charge of the Stakely building now. I think he's hiding something. He seemed nervous."

"Maybe he was nervous because you scared him. You're like a red-headed tank when your mind is set on something."

"Nonetheless, I think he's worth checking out, quietly, of course."

He rolled his eyes. "Oh, of course, because everyone knows it's so easy to keep a secret in this town, especially when someone is investigating the mayor. I don't see that costing me my job at all."

She folded her hands in her lap, pinning him with a stare.

"You don't give up, do you?" he asked after a minute of tense silence.

"No, not ever."

He blew out a breath. "Here's what we're going to do. You're here, and you said someone's been making threats against you."

"I have the license plate of the person who has been following me."

"Give that to me, make a formal statement, and I'll look into it. If that information in any way leads back to the mayor, then I'll have a foundation for an investigation. But I have to be honest with you—as much as I don't want to, I believe Jason is guilty."

"If you'll promise to keep an open mind while you look into things, then that's all I could ask. But I have to be honest with you—unless your investigation clears Jason, then I plan to hire a private detective to look into both cases. There's something I'm missing here, and I'm not going to stop until I figure out what it is."

"That's pretty much what I thought you would say." He reached into his desk and pulled out a piece of paper. "Here's a statement form. Fill out everything that has happened concerning the threats you've received, as well as any other witnesses we might be able to contact. Make sure and sign your name at the bottom and leave it with dispatch. I'll let you know what I find."

Lacy knew she was dismissed. She took the paper from his desk and turned to go, pausing in the doorway. "Thank you, detective," she said, and this time she really meant it.

He nodded and dropped his gaze to his desk, resuming whatever he had been working on before she showed up.

Keegan was still waiting patiently in the lobby, a book in his hands.

"Thanks for waiting," Lacy said.

He looked up at her with a heart-stopping smile and she wondered, not for the first time, what he was doing spending all his time with her this week. "No problem," he said. "Learn anything useful?"

"No, but I made some amends, I suppose. I can check one enemy off my list."

"Two because one got shot," he pointed out.

She wrinkled her nose. "Thanks for reminding me."

He laughed and rested his arm companionably on her shoulders. "What now?"

She checked her watch. "Now we go home and let grandma feed us. I know she's worried. Prepare to eat a lot. You're not diabetic, are you?"

"Not yet, but check back after I leave this week. How is it that you're not five hundred pounds?"

"One of life's little mysteries, and a whole lot of exercise."

"What do you do?" he asked as he opened the passenger door of his rental car.

"I run, if you could call it that. Technically I think it's more like a fast waddle."

"Want to run with me? It might help clear your head."

"I guess we could, but I have to warn you it's not pretty."

"I find that really hard to believe, Lacy, because I haven't seen anything you do that isn't pretty." When he added another smile, she was almost certain he was flirting with her. Was that what this week was about? Was it some elaborate conquest for him? He was sweet in the same way Tosh was sweet, but there was something else going on with him, and she didn't know what. The not knowing was putting her on edge as she waited for the other shoe to drop. After spending so much time together the last few days, she wasn't sure how forceful her protest would be if he tried to make a move on her. Did he know, and was he purposely breaking down her defenses? Or was she being paranoid?

Speaking of paranoid, "I think I made a kid and a grown man wet their respective pants this morning."

"What?" he said, jerking the wheel slightly as he turned to look at her. He was already smiling in anticipation of the story to come, and when she told him how she had terrorized the driving student and his instructor, he bent over the steering wheel laughing. Thankfully, they were in her grandmother's driveway at that point, so there was no chance of him wrecking.

"You are exactly what the doctor ordered," he said.

"Keegan, what does that mean? I know we don't know each other that well, but we've spent a lot of time together the last few days, and I can tell something is going on with you. If you want to talk about it, then I'm here. It's important to me that you know that."

"I appreciate that, Lacy, and I might take you up on it." He reached over the seat and took her hand. "It's a precarious situation with Tosh and our history, you know?"

She nodded, though she didn't know. What was he talking about?

"It might help if I told you. Maybe after we run." He gave her hand a squeeze.

She gave him a lame smile in return. Whatever it was, she wasn't sure she wanted to know anymore. "I wasn't kidding before. I'm not a graceful runner."

"Now I'm intrigued. Go get changed so I can see for myself."

Lacy complied because if he was interested in her, there was no better way for his attraction to die then to see her in her workout gear.

CHAPTER 20

"Wow, that was…something."

Lacy would have responded, but she was still in that phase where she was bent over, trying to breathe.

"Did you ever think there might be something seriously wrong with you?"

She looked up enough to glare at him.

"I'm serious. That wasn't normal looking. Or sounding. Do you have asthma?"

She shook her head. "I'm not athletic, okay?"

"I've run with people who aren't athletes before. It was never like that."

Yes, any attraction on his part was definitely dead now. "C'mon, I need to shower," she said, standing upright as they walked the last few feet to home.

"Okay, but if you feel dizzy or faint in the shower, then you should sit down. I'm pretty sure you were hyperventilating that last mile or so."

While he, of course, hadn't broken a sweat or wheezed once as he easily kept pace with her.

"Maybe you should join a gym, get a trainer—someone professional who is equipped to deal with your particular special needs," he suggested.

She couldn't reply with a snide comeback, both because she was still out of breath and because he sounded sincere. He wasn't making fun of her; he was actually concerned for her wellbeing.

"It's not that big of a deal," she insisted. "I didn't start running until later in life. Lots of people aren't good at running."

"I once saw a story about an army vet who lost both legs in the war, and he still ran better than you do," Keegan said.

Now he was teasing her, and she shoved at him. He grabbed her around the neck in a loose chokehold.

"Shut it, Underwood. And don't tell Tosh. Forget what you've seen here," she said.

"If only I could, but I'm pretty sure the image is burned into my retinas for all of eternity. On my deathbed, I'll probably see the vision of you trying to break a twelve minute mile."

"Keep it up, and we can test that theory really soon," she said, and he laughed. He waited in the kitchen talking to her grandmother while Lacy showered. He didn't need a shower because he still looked and smelled as fresh as a daisy after their—slow, according to him— three mile run.

They ate supper with her grandparents. The meal and conversation was enjoyable, but something was missing, and Lacy knew what it was. Keegan was sweet, interesting, and fun, but he wasn't Tosh. She missed Tosh; where was he?

After supper, Keegan and Lacy transitioned to the living room while her grandparents went out. They sat on the couch, and Keegan picked up her hand and stared at it while he spoke. "Lacy, earlier in the car, you said you wanted to hear what's been on my mind."

Lacy felt a cold pinprick of fear, the same one she felt whenever anyone of the male persuasion wanted to talk about his feelings. *Think of a way to stall.* "Wait," she blurted, and he looked up at her in surprise. "I, um, was wondering if maybe we could go to the Stakely building and have a look around."

"Now?" He glanced out the window at the setting sun.

"That's what flashlights are for. It's just that I saw the sketch from the Pendergast trial of where the shooting took place, and I want to try and pinpoint where it happened while it's fresh in my mind."

"Okay," he drawled. "Let's go to the Stakely building."

His ready agreement made Lacy feel guilty. "Maybe we can talk later." Maybe she would be ready by then to hear whatever it was he had to say.

He nodded and held the door for her, but his smile looked relieved, which increased her guilt. Obviously whatever he had to say was difficult for him, and she wasn't making it any easier. She put her hand on his arm to stop him. "We can stay here. We can talk." *I can act like a grownup and listen to what you have to say without focusing on myself.*

"We'll talk later," he said. "I'm interested to see where the shooting took place. I have to admit that when I left Chicago, the last thing I expected was to get dragged into the middle of a murder investigation."

"I'm sorry. I know this week hasn't been what you envisioned."

"What I envisioned was sitting around Tosh's apartment, counting his show choir trophies, and wondering if he's really my brother. This is so much better it's off the scale."

The ride to the Stakely building only took a couple of minutes. Lacy had grabbed her Grandpa Craig's old flashlight from the shelf in the closet. It was huge, but powerful. There was some residual light from the outside, and if they hurried, they might be able to make it without needing to use the giant flashlight. She unlocked the door and led the way inside, stopping near a beam about a third of the way into the cavernous space.

"If I read the article correctly, then Susan's store was right here. She was shot as she was leaving, so she would have been standing right here." She pivoted so that she was facing Keegan, the beam to her right. "I've never been very good at physics or geometry or whatever you need to figure out trajectory. If the shooter was standing about where you are, where might the bullet have gone when it left her body?"

"So, I'm the shooter," Keegan said. He raised his hands and pressed his index fingers together, pointing them at her like a gun. "If I were a bullet, where would I go?"

Lacy shuddered. It was darker in the building than she had imagined it would be and the junk lying haphazardly created a jumbled disarray of shadows. "This is sort of creepy. Maybe we should come back in the daytime."

"You're not turning chicken on me now, are you?" Keegan asked. He smiled and the shadows behind him seemed to take form and move. Lacy watched, horrified, as the butt of a gun emerged from the shadows and crashed down on his head. He slumped to the floor unconscious. Detective Brenner stepped over his inert body, palming his gun and turning it so it was now facing Lacy.

"I own this building," she said stupidly. "I'm not trespassing."

"I know. You told me today. You remember, it was right about the time you said you weren't going to stop digging until you found out the truth about the murders."

"Are you saying you killed Ed McNeil and Susan Pendergast?"

He didn't respond, but she took the fact that he was still holding a gun on her as a yes.

"And you're here now because you're worried I'm going to find the bullet and it's going to match the gun that was used to kill Ed McNeil?"

"No. That's probably the stupidest proposition I've ever heard. What are the chances that you're going to find that bullet? And, even if you do, the gun is long since gone. It's not like we keep the same guns for twenty-something years."

"Then why are you doing this?"

"Because I know you meant it when you said you won't stop until you find some answers. If you had let it lie, then everyone would have been happy."

"Except for Jason who will rot in jail for a crime he didn't commit," she said.

He shrugged. "What judge won't go easy on a kid like that? An overachiever with a sad childhood; he'll have the jury eating out of his hand. He'll basically get a slap on the wrist and be out in a few years."

"So it was all an act, this pretend like and respect you have for him." *Stall, stall, stall.* She had no idea why she was stalling since she had no plan of escape, but she felt the need to keep him talking nonetheless, and he seemed happy to comply.

"No. I do like Jason, and I meant what I said. He's a good kid and a good officer."

"What, then, you're jealous because he's better at his job than you are?"

He gave a short, humorless chuckle. "You don't think we all start out like Jason, all starry-eyed dreamers intent on saving the world? I was once like him, and then I killed a woman and everything changed."

"Why did you kill her? What did she do to you?"

"Nothing. That's the joke of it. I was here because, with all the drug activity, we were supposed to be keeping an eye on things. I was a fresh-faced wunderkind like your boyfriend, checking the building like a good little soldier, when Susan stepped out of her store and surprised me. I thought everyone had gone home, and I was startled. I didn't even know I had my gun out until she dropped and I saw it in my hands. I panicked."

"And you framed Joe Anton to take the fall?" Lacy asked.

"No. I called Ed McNeil and asked him to go with me as I turned myself in. It was Ed who told me not to do it. He said it wasn't worth losing my career over. I thought he was doing me a favor, but it turned out that he was finding leverage. Didn't you ever wonder why he won so many cases when he wasn't a very good lawyer or why I couldn't have cared less about doing any real investigative work? It's because the entire system is rigged by guys like Ed. Guilt, innocence, it doesn't matter."

"But I don't understand why you waited so long to frame Joe Anton," Lacy said.

"The blackmail went on for years, and I was tired of it. I thought if the case was closed, then Ed would get off my back. I sweated a few bullets when he took Anton's case because I knew he could prove that the man didn't do it. You'll never know how much he tortured me during that trial. I should have killed him then, especially because it didn't work. In fact, things got worse after the trial. Then your article came out, and I knew I was going to be under a lot of scrutiny, so it was time to get rid of Ed."

"Joe Anton said he gave the police a receipt that proved his alibi for the time of the murder," Lacy said.

"He did. I destroyed it, altered the evidence, and set out a trail that led right to Anton. I knew your boy would follow it like the eager beaver he was, and I was correct."

"Then how did you frame Jason?" she asked.

"I switched our guns. The ballistics are correct, but it wasn't Jason's gun they tested; it was mine."

"So, you're just going to shoot us? Don't you think that might be suspicious, especially with Jason in jail? What are you going to do, frame someone else?"

"Yes, as a matter of fact I am. True to my word, I did some investigating on the license plate you gave me. Turns out it comes back to the developers who were so eager to buy this building. They, the mayor, and Ed McNeil had a lucrative little deal going where they would buy the building for a pittance, build a bunch of cheap stores, and sell them for ten times what they paid. Even if I can't make the connection between the developers and the mayor, I can still make it look like they did this, especially when I burn down the building. Fire is so good at destroying forensic evidence. Sometimes knowledge is a powerful weapon, you know?"

The moon slipped from behind a cloud and illuminated the ring on his pinky finger. "You made a mistake. You took Ed McNeil's ring when you killed him," she said.

"This isn't Ed's ring; this is mine."

"You guys had matching rings? That's, uh, nice, I guess. Weird, but, okay."

"We're not the only people in town who have these rings, and there's nothing nice about them."

"What do you mean?" Lacy asked.

"Ding, your time is up," the detective said. He took a step closer and Keegan sprang up out of nowhere, knocking the detective aside. They didn't pause to see if he dropped his gun, instead Keegan took Lacy's hand and dragged her behind him.

Instead of dashing toward the door and freedom, he led her toward the stairs. She tugged on his hand. "Wrong way," she yelled.

"Trust me," he said, not turning around or slowing down. Since she had no choice, and since the detective was gaining on them, she picked up the pace and followed after him, sprinting up the stairs as fast as he did.

They reached the roof and he kicked open the sometimes sticky door. "Step exactly where I step, okay?" he said.

She nodded and then concentrated on looking down, placing her feet exactly where his had been. His steps were large and measured, and she guessed he was stepping on beams.

They were almost at the edge of the roof when the detective appeared behind them, panting from his labored run up four flights of stairs. He paused in the doorway to get his breath and his bearings before raising his gun.

"You can't really think you're going to hit us from over there," Keegan said, and his tone was taunting. "Are you a sharpshooter, detective? Not to mention all the questions multiple shots would raise in the neighborhood. You know from up here they're going to echo."

His taunts seemed to be working because the detective was coming closer. Keegan and Lacy backed up a step. "That's far enough," Keegan said. "Come closer, and we'll go over the side and down the fire escape."

"There's no fire escape up here," Lacy blurted.

Keegan gave her a look and the detective laughed, advancing again. "Oh, Lacy, sometimes you're so unbelievably stupid," he said. He was only fifteen feet away now and closing fast. He raised his gun, and then he was gone, along with about half the roof. Lacy and Keegan picked their way across the beams, standing at the edge of the gaping hole to look down.

The moon illuminated the detective, lying on his back and staring up at them, still alive but groaning in pain, and no wonder. His leg and arm were twisted at an impossible angle, and there was a splinter of wood sticking up through his side. The gun was nowhere in sight, but they still backed away as Lacy pulled out her phone and dialed 911.

CHAPTER 21

Keegan sat on the cot, holding tightly to Lacy's hand while the doctor prepared to stitch his head. He had at first refused an ambulance for the angry-looking gash, but the officers who first showed up at the scene explained that it would take a lot less time waiting in the emergency room if he simply gave in and rode in the ambulance. Lacy had ridden with him, abandoning his rental car for later retrieval.

The ride had been silent as they clasped hands and attempted to process all that had happened. Now, however, Keegan looked ready to talk.

"Lacy," Keegan began, gripping her hand tighter. "I need to finish telling you what I started to tell you earlier."

"Maybe it could wait until later," Lacy said, darting a not so subtle look at the eavesdropping doctor.

"No, it can't wait. I've got to get this out before I go. There's something I need to tell you."

Lacy squeezed her eyes shut, both to block out the sight of the needle heading toward Keegan's head and the words she didn't want to hear. She couldn't add another man into the mix, and especially not this one. Keegan plunged ahead, rambling about life in general while

Lacy plotted her response. *I don't see you as more than a friend.* Or maybe she could use her failsafe: *I could never date Tosh's brother.*

"Wait, what?" she said as his words finally registered.

Keegan took a deep breath and said it again. "I'm going to be a priest."

Lacy stared at him, not blinking until he gave her hand a squeeze. "You're the first person I've told, so it would be really great if you said something right now," he said.

"I'm sorry," she said, shaking her head to clear it. "It's just that there's a little voice in my head that keeps saying 'four days spent with you, and the man is sprinting toward lifelong celibacy,' and the voice sounds suspiciously like my mother."

He laughed, wincing as the stitches pulled. "It has nothing to do with you. Well, it does, but not the way you think." Noting her horrified expression, he hastened to continue. "I've been feeling the call for a while now, but it's not the easiest thing. So I ran. Only apparently I'm Jonah and this is my Nineveh because as we were in the building and that guy was trying to kill us, all I could think was that Someone was definitely trying to tell me something. So I gave in and said yes, and the peace was immediate. Of course, that could be because I was knocked unconscious, but I'm pretty sure it was the priest thing."

"I think you'll be a really great priest, Keegan," Lacy said sincerely. She put her arm around his shoulders and gave them a squeeze. The doctor finished the stitches and slipped away, closing the curtain behind him.

"Do you really?" Keegan asked. The blatant insecurity in his tone was endearing. By now Lacy knew there weren't many things Keegan was insecure about.

"Maybe the best ever. You're going to give the pope a run for his money."

Keegan chuckled uneasily. "Spoken like a true protestant."

They sat in comfortable silence for a few beats until Lacy spoke again. "Not to be totally shallow and self absorbed, but I can't help notice that in the last few days one man has tried to kill me while I've sent another to the priesthood. Not a great week for my self esteem."

Keegan laughed and slipped his arm around her waist, giving it a squeeze. "You want to know something that might help? I was thinking I should have one last kiss before I go, one kiss to last me through all of eternity, and I think that kiss should be with you."

"So now I'm supposed to kiss you, and it's either supposed to be so good that the memory will linger until you die, or so bad that you'll willingly renounce women forever."

He nodded. "No pressure."

Lacy laughed and slid off the cot. "If I'm going to do this, I'm going to do it right. No awkward angles for the man of the cloth." She stood in front of him, thinking the possibility of a no-strings kiss sounded pretty good, even if it was uncharacteristic for her. Unlike with Tosh and Jason, she didn't have to think about a past, present, or future with Keegan. She only had to concentrate on this one moment. She also liked the fact that Keegan was just sitting there smiling at her, allowing her to make the first move.

She cupped his face in her hands, closed her eyes, and kissed him. And kissed him, and kissed him. Apparently the flip side of a kiss without forethought was that it could easily take on a life of its own. At last they broke apart, and Keegan rested his forehead on hers, breathing hard.

"Okay, new plan. Forget the priesthood and Tosh, and we go to Vegas and get married. Right now. Tonight."

Lacy laughed and stepped away. "I feel bad enough I've sent a man into the ministry. I'm not going to be responsible for bringing him back out again."

"That was, well, that was just really wow, Lacy. Thanks. It's going to take me a while to forget about that kiss."

"As penance, every time you think of it you can give a dollar to the poor," Lacy suggested.

"By the time I stop thinking about it, those poor are going to be so stinking rich," he said, and they laughed together. "So, I guess that was my last official act as a layman. Now I'm going to make my first official act as a priest in training." He settled his hands on her shoulders and looked deep into her eyes. "You need to make a decision soon because you have two good men dangling on the line. Cut one of them loose, or cut them both loose, but don't leave them hanging."

"How do I know which one?"

"That's the part only you can answer. I think you know which one I want you to choose, but I also want you to be happy, to do what's best for you. Only you can figure out what that is."

Lacy nodded. "Thank you, Father Keegan."

Keegan shuddered and dropped his hands. "I wonder how long it's going to take before that stops freaking me out."

They both turned to look as the curtain beside them was roughly jerked aside. Tosh stood there, scowling as his eyes darted between them.

"I'm okay. Lacy's good, too. Thanks for asking," Keegan said.

"Oh, yeah, well, you know," Tosh muttered. "Are you good to go, or do we need to wait around some more?"

"I'm good," Keegan said. "And we're giving Lacy a ride."

"Oh," Tosh said, clearly uncomfortable with that idea. Before Lacy could try to respond, she heard the familiar voice of her grandfather at the nurse's station, and even from so far away she could tell he was upset.

She stepped outside of the curtain and saw him leaning toward the nurse, speaking imploringly. "Grandpa," Lacy said, so overwhelmed with joy and relief at the sight of him that she didn't at first realize she had overcome her stumbling block and called him something other than "Hey" or "You."

He realized, though, as he turned to her with a smile that was a mixture of delight, relief, and worry. He opened his arms to her and she tripped into them, being careful not to knock him over when she returned his hug. She needn't have worried, though. He was surprisingly solid for someone in his seventies. When his arms wrapped around her and squeezed, strong and secure, she felt six instead of twenty six.

"Okay?" he asked.

She nodded against his chest, not wanting to speak for the moment.

"I'll take her home," she heard him say to Tosh and Keegan.

She looked up to see Tosh staring at her, perplexed. Keegan grabbed his arm and wrenched it behind his back. "C'mon, Pastor," he said. "You and I are going to have a little talk."

She watched them walk away and her grandfather released her from his embrace, settling his arm around her shoulders. "Ready to go home?" he asked. "Your grandmother is baking."

"Your grandmother is baking" was their code for "your grandmother is worried sick." "Poor Grandma," Lacy said, feeling bad that she had caused her grandparents so much worry lately.

"She's fine," her grandfather said, giving her shoulders a bracing squeeze.

"Because she has you taking care of her," Lacy said. "I'm so glad for you, Grandpa." It was funny how once she finally said the name she had no trouble repeating it. "Grandma's always been so stalwart, but I guess I never realized how much she was hiding. Since you've come along, she's more settled, more peaceful, and definitely happier. It's nice." She smiled, picturing the sweet look her grandparents reserved for each other.

"Your grandma is a great lady, Lacy. I'm the one who's lucky."

As much as Lacy was happy for them, there was always a little bit of wistfulness thrown in. Would she ever find what they had? And would she find it before she was seventy? She hoped so.

"So tell me all about it," her grandfather commanded, and she spent the ride home doing just that.

As soon as she arrived home and assured her grandmother that she was all right, she called Travis and filled him in on the night's events, knowing he would get the trickle down effect the next morning when the news reached the jail.

"I wish I could say we could let Jason out right now, but you know how it works. We have to receive the official word from the prosecutor," he said. "I'm so glad it's over, and glad you're okay."

"Me, too. Thanks for everything, Travis. Thanks for your help, and thanks for believing in Jason."

"What I'm about to say is going to sound corny, and if you ever tell him I said so, then I will deny it, but Jason is one of the good guys, and everybody needs someone to look up to, you know?"

"I do know," Lacy said because she felt the same way. Jason was one of the good ones.

"So I guess I'll see you when you come to pick him up," Travis said.

Lacy hadn't thought of that. Would she be the one who was there when he got out of jail? "I guess you will," she said. They said goodbye and disconnected.

She felt gritty, and her exhaustion was bone deep, but she still couldn't shower or go to bed. First she had to turn on her laptop and write the promised article for the paper. She mailed it to Len, along with the instruction to check it carefully for typos because she was so tired, and then finally, she turned on the hot water and stepped blissfully beneath the spray.

CHAPTER 22

Lacy had just showered and changed into her pajamas when a knock sounded at her door. The knock was so insistent she thought it must be Jason; he was usually the only one so desperate to see her, and usually his desperation was caused by worry or anger. She knew it wasn't Jason, though, because Jason hadn't been released yet.

Her grandmother was already in bed, after having baked an apple cake that she practically spoon fed to Lacy upon her return home. Not that it had taken much coaxing to get Lacy to eat. She made a mental note to run the next day to work off some of the excess calories.

"Tosh," Lacy said, breathless from her sprint down the hall to try and silence the door before it could rouse her grandmother.

"I didn't know what had happened," Tosh blurted. He stepped forward and wrapped her in a hug so tight that he deflated all the air from her lungs. "I'm so sorry. When Keegan called, he said he needed some stitches. He didn't tell me what had happened to you guys, or that you were involved. And then I showed up, and I was such a jerk."

"Can't breathe," Lacy managed to gasp.

"Oh." He let her go and stepped back, looking sad and penitent.

"Tosh, what has been going on this week? Why have you been dodging me?"

"I thought you and Keegan were, you know, into each other."

"Tosh," Lacy said, her tone accusing.

"Lacy, you have to understand the women I like always go for him over me. I've spent most of my life feeling like a consolation prize. Why would I think this time would be any different? And you guys spent so much time together and seemed to be hitting it off. I thought I was doing the honorable thing by bowing out. But he told me about the priest thing, and then I felt like the world's biggest idiot."

"Tosh, that's because you are. I would never, ever, ever do that to you. Don't you understand I know exactly how that feels? Men always prefer Riley to me. Even if Keegan wasn't going to be a priest, he and I would never be anything more than friends. I would never do that to you," she reiterated. "I would never hurt you like that." Somehow during her impassioned speech, he had slipped his arms around her and was now holding her close.

"There's one more thing we need to discuss," he said. "I hate to bring this up when we're on the verge of making amends, but it's something you need to know."

"What?"

"Remember how you've been bugging me to hire a new secretary since Marjory retired?"

"Yes," she said, not sure why his secretary would be an issue between them. "It's about time you found someone. Hopefully this will ease your workload. Who did you get?"

He just looked at her, and somehow she knew.

"You hired Pearl," she said.

He nodded.

She tried to wriggle free of his clasp, but he wouldn't allow it. "How could you hire that woman, Tosh? She hates me, I mean like really and truly hates me."

"I think if you guys got to know each other you might be friends," he said.

"You want me to be friends with the woman who chased me down the street trying to kill me?" she asked.

He nodded again. "She had nowhere else to go, Lacy. She's sad and lonely and practically destitute. What was I supposed to do?"

"Not hire her," Lacy suggested.

"Fine. I'll call her in the morning and fire her. I'm sure it's not too late for her to get on welfare. Of course, the aging mother she supports will be on her own, but that really isn't our problem."

Lacy pressed her palm over his mouth. "You've made your point. Pearl is a hapless victim of society and it's up to you to save her."

He kissed her hand before she took it away. "Just give her a chance, okay? I think you guys simply got off on the wrong foot. Things will work out—you'll see."

His smile was so warm and infectious that she found herself smiling in return. "I missed you, Tosh," she said. She hugged him, resting her head against his chest.

"Missed you, too. Sorry I was a jerk." He leaned down to kiss the top of her forehead.

"That's it?" They turned to see Keegan with his head out the window, staring at them. "You haven't spoken in a week, and that's how you make up? That's pathetic. Kiss the woman, Tosh. Trust me when I tell you that you won't regret it."

"This is awkward," Lacy said.

"Can you imagine him as someone's priest?" Tosh said.

"About as well as I can imagine you as someone's pastor," she replied. She hugged him, standing on her toes to kiss his cheek. "Call me."

"I will," Tosh promised solemnly. "I'll have my new secretary make a note. She'll be thrilled—she's a big fan of yours."

"Hilarious," Lacy said. "It's all fun and games until I end up locked in Pearl's closet, living on a steady diet of stale bridge mix and recycled cat water."

Tosh laughed and reciprocated the cheek kiss. Turning, he jogged to his car. Lacy remained on the porch, waving to Keegan as he blew her a kiss. Tosh paused, looking between them with a puzzled frown.

Lacy smiled at him, shrugging, and he finally got in his car and drove away.

* * *

The next morning, the jangling of her phone startled Lacy from some much needed sleep.

"It's Travis," he said without preamble. "They're releasing Jason in an hour. I thought you'd want to know."

"I do," she assured him in a gravelly croak. "Thanks, Travis. You're the best."

Lacy closed her phone and jumped into the shower, determined to look good for the upcoming encounter with Jason. Forty five minutes later, she was clean and polished, and looking more like she was going on a fancy date than picking up a friend from jail.

She borrowed her grandmother's car, but then a new thought struck her. What if he already had someone lined up to retrieve him from jail? They hadn't been on the best of terms lately. Would he be glad to see her? Would she be humiliated if there was another car and another woman waiting to pick him up? They had never talked about the other women he saw, but Lacy knew they existed. A band of anxiety settled around her chest as she debated with herself about turning the car around. Part of her felt like she was doing the right thing—someone needed to be there for Jason to show him she cared. The other part of her felt foolish and vulnerable for taking such a big step uninvited. Would he turn her away?

Unfortunately she arrived with ten minutes to spare. The extra time did nothing to ease her anxiety. She drummed her fingers impatiently on the steering wheel, still trying to decide if she was going to turn tail and run. Just as she made up her mind to bolt, the jail doors opened, and Jason stepped out.

Lacy's heart squeezed at the sight of him. He looked tired and, even worse, alone. She opened the car door and took a step out. The sound caught his attention and he looked at her. He stopped walking.

For a split second, they remained frozen, staring at each other. And then he smiled.

Lacy smiled in return and began walking toward him. He resumed his steps, his pace much faster now. By the time she reached him, she was sprinting. He caught her and picked her up, enveloping her in his arms as he spun her in a tight circle. His face pressed to her neck and inhaled.

"Are you okay?" she asked, her voice a shaky whisper.

"I'm good," he assured her. The sound was muffled by her clavicle.

Her fingers plunged into his hair, holding him close. She hadn't admitted even to herself how afraid she had been this week. What if things hadn't worked out? She might never have seen him again. They were making a small scene on the sidewalk, but neither cared.

Jason eased away from her slightly so he could see her face, but he didn't set her down. Her feet dangled off the ground, her toes skimming the pavement. "Thanks for getting me out, Red."

She smiled. "You're not still mad I meddled?"

"Livid," he assured her. "But I'm also grateful. Later, once the euphoria has worn off, I'll punish you most severely for almost getting yourself killed again." The way his eyes gleamed when he talked about her punishment made her want to melt, but she held herself in check.

"I knew you didn't do it, Jason," she said. She pressed her palm to his cheek and smiled when he rubbed his stubbly face against it.

"You're the only one who believed in me," he said. "The town was ready to string me up."

"Not true," she said. "You shouldn't listen to the vocal minority. Lots of people had their doubts. And lots of people believed for sure you were innocent." He gave her a dubious look, and she continued. "My grandparents believed in you. So did Travis. Even Tosh had his doubts."

His brow crinkled at the mention of Tosh, but then he smiled and shook his head. His eyes skimmed her face, tracing her features. "I can't seem to get enough of you, Red. Why is that?"

"I don't know," she said peevishly, irritated by his grudging tone.

"Even when I want to throttle you I want to..." He let the thought trail off. "Anyway, I had a lot of time to think while I was in jail. I've decided to make peace with the times I don't want to wring your neck."

"What does that mean?" she asked.

He didn't answer. Instead, his eyes caught hers and held, making her squirm with his unspoken meaning. Nervously, she cleared her throat. "Are you up for an adventure?"

His arm tightened on her waist, and Lacy realized he was still holding her aloft. "What kind of adventure?" he whispered.

Aware that they were quickly in danger of becoming a public spectacle, Lacy wriggled away from him until he set her down. "I want you to come see my building."

"What building?" His puzzled frown reminded her that she had forgotten to tell him.

"I bought the Stakely building."

He turned to look at the jail. "How long was I in there?"

She laughed and grasped his hand. "Too long. Come on." She was practically giddy with relief. Jason was free, and he was happy to see her. Beyond that, she didn't want to figure anything out, but apparently Jason did. He stilled her hand when she attempted to start the car.

"You keep running from me," he said. "Every time it seems like we're making progress, taking a step forward, getting close to…something, you sprint in the opposite direction like ghosts are chasing you. After everything we've been through the last few weeks, I want to know why. I think I deserve to know why."

She took a deep breath that was supposed to be steadying but instead sounded shaky. Her gaze focused on a squashed bug on the windshield. "I don't love easily, Jason. I don't open myself up or let go of my hard-earned control. I'm not the person who flits from relationship to relationship, from man to man. I don't let people in and let them get close to me. And when I do, it's like I'm stuck on them forever, you know? The guy, my fiancé, Robert, the reason I left New York. I thought he was the one; I gave him everything without reserve. He crushed me."

"Lacy." She turned to look at him. "I'm sorry you were hurt, truly." He reached out and brushed a finger tenderly on her cheek. "But I'm not him."

Why was it so easy to tell Tosh she wasn't ready for commitment and so difficult to tell Jason? Maybe because Tosh didn't look at her with the same intensity. Jason, with his dark hair, kaleidoscope eyes, and roguish beard stubble, looked like a wayward pirate. His devilish good looks, combined with the tender tone he was now using, were almost too much for Lacy to resist.

"In my head, I know that. But the heart is another matter entirely. You are…not safe."

His eyes blinked with hurt he tried and failed to disguise. "Why not?"

"A number of reasons. Mostly because you look like you do, but also because of the way things were in high school."

"I'm not the same person I was then, and neither are you."

"Again, the head and the heart differ on reality there. But what it comes down to is this: the reason I keep insisting we're only friends is because I'm not ready; I'm not whole, and as deep as the wound is, I don't know if I ever will be. I wish I could blink it all away and say I'm healed and ready to move on, but I'm not wired that way. Things go deep with me, all the way to the heart, and right now my heart is in tatters. All I can do is try to protect it and hope someday…" Lacy trailed off. She wanted to imagine a someday, but she couldn't quite picture it. Someday with Jason Cantor felt far too scary to contemplate. He could hurt her; he could break her. If that happened, she knew she would never get over him, never recover. He didn't reply. The intense silence made her nervous. "You don't want commitment, either," she reminded him, poking his bicep to try and lighten the somber mood of the car.

There was another long pause before he answered. "That's always been my motto," was his cryptic reply.

"Can't we enjoy whatever is between us without putting labels or constraints on it?" she asked.

Again he took a long time to answer. "Lacy, when you run, it makes me want to pursue." His mouth spread into a slow smile. "And I like chasing you."

Lacy watched, mesmerized, as he slowly leaned in and kissed her. The press of his lips on hers jogged her out of her trance, and she responded full force as she always did when he touched her, sliding her arms around him and jabbing her fingers into his ridiculous hair. Eventually, he pulled himself away and tried to steady his ragged breathing. He rested his forehead on her shoulder.

"Dang, Lacy, for someone who doesn't want commitment, you sure kiss like you mean business."

"You have that effect on me," she said before she could think of something less revealing to say.

He laughed, and the low rumbling sound went straight to her gut, causing it to clench and pitch. She rolled her eyes. Apparently even his voice had an effect on her.

"The feeling is mutual," he assured her.

"But, Jason..." she began, but he interrupted

"We're friends, only friends. I get it. Consider that a kiss hello. In Europe, they do it all the time," he said.

She grinned at him. "I definitely feel like I've been to France."

He laughed before pulling away and sitting up. "Let's go see your building, pal."

The ride to the Stakely building was silent, but the silence was comfortable. Jason smiled when they pulled up in the parking lot, staring at the building, *her* building.

"I can't believe you bought this thing," he said.

"They were going to tear it down," she said defensively.

"And you're the patron saint of lost causes." The way he said it, then leaned over and caressed her cheek again, made her wonder if he was referring to more than the building. But surely he wasn't talking about himself, was he? Jason was anything but a lost cause.

"Come inside," she invited.

"Are we sure it's safe?" he asked.

"Don't make fun of my building. I had it inspected, and it's thoroughly safe as long as you don't use the wiring, plumbing, wood floors, or roof," she answered, suppressing the unpleasant memories from the night before.

"What exactly can we do in there?" he asked, eyeing the building with suspicion.

"Anything we want," she said. Tugging his hand impatiently, she led him behind her into the building. "Isn't it beautiful?" she asked as they stepped through the entryway. The sight of those two open floors never failed to inspire her.

"Uh, sure," Jason said unconvincingly.

She wheeled on him, hands on hips. "You have to use your imagination, spoilsport." She put her arm around his waist, drawing him farther into the room. "Picture a market with every imaginable merchant. Restaurants will fill the air with savory scents, and people will come to shop and mingle. There can be flower stalls and a bakery, maybe even an art gallery or two."

"Sounds super," he said with forced enthusiasm.

She tried to give his waist a painful squeeze, but she was sure he barely felt it. "You're not even trying."

He smiled down at her and put his arms around her, returning her squeeze. "You're right, I'm sorry. Try again. Tell me how amazing it's going to be."

"You're making fun of me," she accused.

He shook his head. "I'm not. I'm not as visionary as you are, but when you say it, I can almost picture it."

"You have to withhold judgment until you see the entire space. Let's go upstairs." She tugged him toward the stairwell.

"Can't we take the elevator?" he asked.

"Only if we want to plummet," she said.

"Stairs it is," he agreed, opening the door and holding it wide while she preceded him inside. Lacy paused at the base of the stairs and looked up.

"Four floors," she whispered.

"Where's all that enthusiasm for the new space?" he asked.

"Not in my calves," she replied.

"Do you want me to carry you?" he asked.

Lacy laughed.

"Why do you think I'm joking? I'll carry you," he said.

"Jason, it's four flights, and I'm not exactly weightless," she said.

He inspected her, taking her measure.

"Okay, that's enough. It's like you're an undertaker measuring me for my coffin," she said.

"Lacy, I'm in the best shape of my life. I think you underestimate my lifting capacity."

"I think you underestimate my ability to suck in and wear figure flatting clothes." She punched his arm. "Stop looking at my body."

"Stop bringing it to my attention." He turned his back to her. "Hop on."

"Are you sure about this?" she asked.

"Positive." She hopped on his back. He carried her up all four flights of stairs, far faster than she would have made them on her own, not letting her down until they were safely inside the fourth floor. "You did it, that's amazing."

Her congratulations were lost on him as he stared around the cavernous space in wonder. "This is awesome."

Lacy, delighted by his approval, hooked her arm through his and used it to drag him to the floor-to-ceiling windows. "Look at the view."

"It's incredible. This has to be the best space in the city. When are you moving in?" he asked.

"Um, probably the fifth day of never," Lacy said.

"What? You're seriously not going to live here?" he asked, incredulous.

"It's going to take me so long and cost so much money to renovate the other parts of the building; I have no idea when or how I'm ever going to get to this. Plus I have no idea what to do with it. And it's so…cavernous."

"I know, but it's amazing. You could put the kitchen over there," he dragged her to a spot on the far side of the room. "The bedrooms could go there, and all this space could be open concept. Look at the exposed brick. You could go full-on industrial."

"Why don't you move in here?" she suggested.

"I don't think I could afford this place," he said.

"Like I would charge you," she said.

"I can't live in your building rent-free," he said.

Why not? You already live in my head that way. "You totally could. It's going to go to waste otherwise, or get crowded with junk and storage."

"That would feel weird," he said.

"Fine, I'll charge you."

"How much?" he asked. Was he seriously considering her offer?

"A hundred million dollars," she said.

"Thanks for keeping it affordable," he said.

"I'm sure we could come to some kind of agreement, whenever it eventually gets finished," Lacy said.

"I might hold you to that," Jason said, still staring around the space.

"Come on, I'll show you the third floor. It's not as exciting, but it's where the money is. I plan to have offices and lots of renters."

"One question, Red," he said after she finished the tour and they returned to the first floor. "Where are you going to get these phantom tenants?"

"Actually," she began. She checked his watch, squinting against the darkness. "I'm supposed to be meeting one here today."

As if prompted by her words, the front door squeaked open, and a tentative voice called out a greeting.

"Hello," Lacy said. "Come in, we're in here." At her grandfather's suggestion, she had put out an ad for artists and entrepreneurs who might be willing to open a store in the market as soon as it was remodeled in a few months. So far she'd had one response, the person she was meeting with today.

The woman stepped into view, looking like the type of woman Lacy had suspected would open a bead shop—tall, blond, and attractive. She had been skeptical that a bead store could make it, but the woman had explained that a lot of people made jewelry as a hobby. In her current location, her store was thriving, but she was looking to make a change and thought the Stakely building sounded ideal.

Lacy let go of Jason and stepped forward, her hand outstretched. "I'm Lacy Steele."

"I'm Cindy…"

"Davenport!"

Both women turned to Jason with surprise when he finished Cindy's greeting for her.

"You know her?" Lacy asked. Her tone dimmed as she took in the way Cindy and Jason were now staring at each other.

"Of course I do," Jason said. "And so do you." He stepped forward and picked Cindy up, twirling her in a circle before returning her to the ground. "I can't believe this."

Lacy frowned. "What do you mean I know her?"

Jason finally tore his eyes off Cindy and turned to Lacy, exasperated. "Cindy Davenport," he reiterated. "She was a year ahead of us. She was a cheerleader. She was my girlfriend," he said, giving Cindy a wink and a smile.

Lacy felt a sinking feeling she was sure had nothing to do with her memory lapse. "Oh, okay." In high school, she hadn't paid much attention to the beautiful people, as she had called them. But after Jason jogged her mind, she vaguely remembered peppy and pretty Cindy, who had always hovered near Jason as he walked down the hall. "Super," she added, but neither one paid her any attention because they were still staring at each other.

"Perfect," Cindy said as she beamed at Jason. "This is absolutely perfect. I can't believe you're still here. It's like fate."

"Fate," Jason repeated.

Fate, Lacy decided, needed a big fat fist in the mouth.

Thank you for reading *Building Blocks of Murder*, the second book in the Lacy Steele Mystery Series. For more books, please check out my website at www.vanessagraybartal.com